Maui Time

by

Rohn Alice Federbush

Maui Time

Cover Art by *Lea Schizas*

The Wild Rose Press, Inc.
PO Box 708
Adams Basin, NY 14410-0708
Visit us at www.thewildrosepress.com

Publishing History
First Edition, 2022
Trade Paperback ISBN 978-1-5092-4628-1
Digital ISBN 978-1-5092-4629-8

Published in the United States of America

Dedication

To my silent son, Robert Warner, who instigated a Navy's dependent cruise to the island of Maui…and a submarine ride to the big island.

Instead of heading toward the ocean to gain access to the offices above the Pioneer Inn, I wandered among the tourists on Front Street to sort out my thoughts. None of these people belonged here. I did. I tried to imagine the shoreline sans people, without the buildings. The voices of Lahaina's avid shoppers couldn't drown out the ocean's symphony, but tranquility got lost in the hubbub. Frigid weather on the mainland blossomed tourists under Maui's incessant sun.

Lahaina's Front Street twinkled with Christmas lights. Light posts, even street signs, were festooned with plastic bells and reindeer. The art studios vied with the junk shops for gift dollars. T-shirts, illegal scrimshaw, and imported silk shops; boutiques, leather emporiums; souvenir junk, eel skins, and tattoo parlors outdid each other in garish window decorations inviting prospective Santas to throw away all their money in the twelve days left before Christmas. I blamed my jumpy nerves for my momentary lack of courage. For a further excuse to delay seeking out the investigator's office, I told myself I needed a change of clothing, something that didn't remotely smell like Henry Halloway. I promised myself to return to Front Street on Saturday morning to hire a replacement spy secretary from Clay's agency. Business ethics concerning Halloway's privacy could be set aside, temporarily. Chris Manning needed to be found before another suspicious accident occurred.

Praise for Rohn Alice Federbush

Maui Time was a finalist in the Marlene Contest in 2006.

Chapter One

Sunday, December 9
Maui

On the way up to the peak of Maui's sleeping volcano, Claire Nemish stopped pedaling and pulled her bike to the outside rim of the road. Following behind, Pam O'Brian assumed they were now above the cloud bank of fog, and that Claire had stopped to appreciate the azure ocean. As she slid her bike next to Claire's, a wall of white cloud, which seemed permanently affixed to the winding road, greeted her.

"How much farther?" Pam spaced her words between gasps for air. She knew Claire did not appreciate wimps.

"Water break." Claire slapped Pam's shoulder. "I can't see a blessed thing."

Pam carefully wet the inside of her mouth. She knew she wouldn't be able to refill her water bottle until they reached their destination. Rationing the precious fluid was the only sane thing to do because she couldn't figure out how far they'd come, or how long they would have to bike. "We're walking on clouds." Pam managed to sound upbeat.

These weekly trips to the summit were not nearly as enjoyable as reclining on warm beaches or stretched out on their roof's hammock with a good book.

However; her partner, Claire, demanded they live a healthy life together. "Heaven bound," Claire said before raising her palm. "Do you hear that?"

"Truck," Pam said. "Should we go to the inside of the road?"

"We're safe," Claire said.

Pam inched as close to the rim of the road as possible, but when Claire didn't budge closer, she cautioned, "Move out a little, Claire."

A yellow pickup barreled around the corner from below them. With plenty of room on the inside of the road, the driver seemed intent on staying in their lane. Pam shut her eyes when the truck appeared purposefully to head even closer to them as the driver increased his speed up the steep incline.

"Fool!" Claire's fist rose.

In response, the truck shied playfully in her direction before disappearing into the whiteness.

"Did you get the plate?" Claire asked.

"I didn't think," Pam admitted. "The pickup was yellow, though."

"Leave the bikes." Claire dropped hers.

Pam obediently laid her bike well to the side of the road. "On foot?" she asked before joining her friend.

"We're near the top. We can get that idiot." Running full tilt, Claire huffed, "I don't hear the truck."

"The cloud muffles sounds." Pam barely dragged the words from her laboring lungs. Running uphill was even more difficult than biking in the skimpy oxygen of mountain air.

Thankfully, Claire stopped. "Crouch down. He's already coming back down." They slipped behind a roadside boulder.

Pam clung to the fog-drenched surface. Her feet held tenaciously to the downward slope of the black gravel. A flash of yellow passed, and Claire leaped out onto the road. Too fast, Pam thought. "He'll see you."

"Got it!" Claire sounded triumphant.

Pam heard the screech of brakes. "He's coming back?"

Claire stood in the road. "He can't turn around."

"He could put it in reverse," Pam ventured. Then they heard the noise: metal hitting the resounding steel bed of the pickup.

"He's stealing our bikes!" they said in unison before running back down, toward the sound.

****

Friday, December 14

I checked my pink wristwatch. In Maui time, twenty minutes to nine was early enough. Six months of acclimation as the Director of Personnel taught me not to arrive at eight, way too early to rattle workers who might be a cup-of-coffee shy of peak performance. Maui's humidity and the warm wind played havoc with my red curls. My high heels clicked against marble tiles as I strolled leisurely from the parking lot behind the building to the front entrance of Maui Power's office complex. Fragrant, imported pink rose hedges lined the circular drive in front of the white stone mansion. These flowers and other permanent traces of colonialism washed over my island home like tsunami tidal waves. Accepting reality was the peace-keeping mantra I lived by. Maui's blurred blood lines and the imperatives of international commerce allowed little sway for the individual to control or even claim.

I wondered if Pam O'Brian and Claire Nemish

chose to work for the utility company because of the historic, administration building itself. Off hours, they volunteered for the island's restoration project. They were the first people I hired in a time-share arrangement for the Purchasing Manager. They biked to the power company in Kihei from their apartment in Olowlau.

Unfortunately, as Green Party members, they made weekly complaints about the company's pollution of heated water into Sugar Beach Bay. And they weren't shy about reporting the company's stalled clean-up attempt to mainland newspapers. Last Sunday, their bodies were recovered from a car that plunged off the steep switchback road to Maui's volcanic peak. A week's worth of newspaper articles about Pam and Claire's perplexing accident weighed down my briefcase. I kept thinking if I thoroughly digested the reports, I could make some sense of the curious disaster. I meant to find out why I felt their loss so personally.

My office commanded the first-floor space to the right of the building's columned entrance. New metal detectors were being installed. Maui Power's use of nuclear energy allowed the federal government to demand the installation of protection devices in some useless expenditure against terror.

Liz Cameron, my secretary, flirted with the construction gang while she watered the lobby plants. "Hey, Saint Svetlana," Liz called. "You're in trouble now."

I looked at the toes of my high heels in astonishment. "These shoes just stepped foot on company property." We grinned at each other before she followed me through her office and the second pair of doors to my office. "In trouble, am I?" I laid my heavy briefcase on the desk.

"Chris Manning is missing." Liz politely examined the tips of her long blonde hair for split ends, to allow me a second to react.

"Nonsense," I said, sitting down too quickly. The back of my chair tapped me on the head as a reminder of grace and decorum. "Surely Chris left a message on our machine?" Chris was the chirpy temp from purchasing. "Henry Halloway likes her."

Liz shook her head. "Maybe Chris decided she couldn't stand being around him. Our message system went down last night. The cell phone listed on her application isn't responding. Better take the bull by the horns and meet Halloway in his office." Liz leveled a sympathetic look toward me. "I'd lend you a clothespin if I owned one." She started to leave but paused, both hands on the double doors. "I'll drive by Chris' apartment after work if you want me to."

"I'll handle that," I said, not looking forward to the task.

"While you're damned to spend time before that smelly monster upstairs, could you put in a plug for Christmas decorations? There are only twelve days to Christmas."

"A taste of coffee before I'm gored?" I pleaded.

"You got it." Liz saluted and sauntered out in her silly way, tipping her shoulders from side to side, like a mechanical kewpie doll.

I stalled for as long as I could. Contact with Halloway was never pleasant. He had taken every opportunity during the last six months to communicate directly to me his displeasure with my qualifications. As far as he was concerned, five years of college in Urbana only meant my dad's influence purchased my position. I locked my purse in the bottom drawer of the desk and sipped the rich black coffee that Liz provided. I loved my job. However, not all of the existing personnel at Maui Power met my standards. I respected the people I hired for the company, like the two women who were now dead.

Claire Nemish was older than Pam O'Brian, but both were too young for life to be taken away. I suspected they were both within the four-year span of my high-school career. However, they attended school on the mainland, New Jersey, and New Mexico, I thought. I remembered their joke, calling the island, "New Maui."

Typical environmentalists, they used no deodorant or hair spray. Heaven alone knew what possessed them to finally use a car. The trunk was empty according to the newspapers. Neither woman's purse was found at the accident site. The ownership of the damaged car had not been established, and the island's airport rental companies denied renting a car to the two women. The VIN was surely being tracked down. Strange business for peaceful Maui.

Finished with the last drop of tepid coffee, I stalled by straightening the yellow pillows on the cobalt blue couch. Decorating at my own expense, I hoped the deep red carpet added to the primary color scheme and brought the island's vitality indoors. According to my psychology courses, the bold color choices underscored my lack of confidence. I knew the budget for my department didn't provide for frivolity. I wouldn't waste my breath or time mentioning Christmas to Halloway. Finally, after giving my credit card to Liz for decorations, I marched up the spiral staircase in the center of the two-story foyer. I tried to steel my sense of smell against the expected stench. Good air was a problem around Halloway. Months of chit-chat with Liz failed to uncover the reason for the odor. His thinning black hair was plastered down with something that could have been KY jelly. Whatever the greasy stuff was, it seemed the source of the rancid smell.

Halloway's purchasing office, next to the CEO's, faced the ocean. Our CEO was on vacation through New Year's Day. I sent a fax to his hotel in Las Vegas on Monday with details about the accident. By return fax, he directed me to fill the vacancy immediately with a temporary secretary. Chris Manning lasted as the temp for three days. On her desk, the candles she burned to dispel the lingering odor from her boss were unlit. Against all the safety regulations, I fired up all of them and took a deep breath before knocking on Halloway's door.

"Come in," he called in his usual rough tone.

Besides being ugly, Henry Halloway was fat. Not all over. His arms and legs were skinny, as was his scrawny neck. His tan jacket was unbuttoned and the perfectly round stomach rolled at me, followed by Halloway's yellowed face, grinning stained teeth, and expressionless pupils set in cold amber. "Only need a minute," I said, exhaling a bit of the air I would need to prevent inhaling.

Motioning toward the wall of windows, I stepped around his desk and cranked the old-fashioned knob that opened the window to a supply of fresh air. "Did you see that blue parrot?" I breathed deeply, sighing at an imaginary bird to save his feelings.

"No," Henry grumbled and faced me. His office was entirely tan: the walls, the carpeting, the blond wooden desk. His suit, shirt, and tie, even his shoes were all the same dull shade. Perhaps he thought to blend into his surroundings so no one would notice his strange obesity. "No secretary!" he said. "Again."

"I'll try to find you someone." I stayed near the window replenishing my lungs' supply of untainted air.

"Come over here," he called. "Pick up this pencil. Now try setting the pencil on the desk." I did as told with my mouth shut. "Don't put the pencil on the desk. *Try* putting it on the desk." He took the pencil and suspended it an inch above the desk. "That's trying. Trying accomplishes nothing."

"Of course." I inadvertently inhaled and coughed.

Halloway's disdain dripped from every syllable. "And now I suppose you'll start sniveling like a twenty-six-year-old, privileged brat." He waved his surrounding, noxious aura toward me in a gesture of dismissal. "I know, I know, with a Master's Degree under your belt, your real moral problem remains entrenched."

I could feel my anger rise from the tips of my toes. A nice karate kick to that protruding stomach would stop the blowhard. Instead, I stood my ground, refusing to belittle myself by losing my temper in front of the jerk.

So he continued my instruction. "...you thoroughly enjoy all the amenities of being Kani Nigel's only daughter, don't you?"

Without commenting on the insults from this non-native citizen of Maui, I answered, "I'll make sure your secretarial position is covered by Monday."

"See to it," he said and motioned for me to leave.

Once outside his office, I blew my nose, not caring if Halloway thought I was crying. I wanted to slip off my high heels, run down the slick marble steps, push through the construction gang, stand in the driveway outside, and breathe in the clean ocean air. Instead, I lifted each of the three candles and blew out their flames, one for each secretary eaten by the foul mouth of the monster.

Where was Chris? I went through her desk. Why did she abandon personal belongings: make-up, tennis shoes, cough medicine, extra matches? Halloway's presence required a certain effort but didn't warrant a hasty abandonment of a well-paying job on Maui. I filled a box with Chris' property but left the serviceable candles and matches for the next person to wade into Halloway's chemistry.

Halloway's name sounded like the Hawaiian word, Haole. 'Haole' meant born from no one, an orphan of any native alliance. There was no denying that common usage on the island made the word akin to the slang word for black people on the mainland. I put up with Halloway by believing he might have been victimized as a poor youngster in grammar school. His hatred for me, my mixed-race family, was evident.

When I first arrived on the job, I scanned his files, hoping to talk candidly to a family member about the smell. No personal names were listed in his twenty-year-old application, and not one name showed up in his benefit package. I neither found the standard letters of reference kept in personnel records. Whoever recommended Halloway, and let him keep his job, was a mystery. Halloway was certainly a master of intimidation, and I felt sympathy for the person responsible for keeping Halloway at Maui Power. I failed to mention the odiferous problem to recruits for his secretarial position. They found out soon enough.

I should not have told Liz I didn't need her. Maybe Chris' neighbors would talk easier to two young women. At least, I could find out if Chris was ill. I had planned to use my lunch hour to read through the newspaper accounts of Pam and Claire's accident. Instead, I asked Liz to lunch. "Could we swing by Chris' apartment and then have lunch in Hana?"

"Lunch first." Liz winked at me.

Once at Chris' address in Hana, the landlady opened the apartment's office door to shout, "Alzheimer's," at us over the screams of an older woman, punctuating the air from a back bedroom. Then she stepped out into the hall and closed the door on the horrors within.

Liz spoke first. "Does she attack you?"

The woman put both her hands in her hair as if to make herself presentable. "Of course not. Who told you that?"

"My mother's dog suffered from dementia and tried to bite her," Liz said.

"I'm so sorry," the landlady and I said.

A fresh set of screams started, accompanied by crashing furniture. "Is there something you need, Svetlana?" A desperate look flickered and was gone. "I should get back to my mother."

"So sorry," I said quickly to let her return to the growing pandemonium behind the door. "It's just that we haven't heard from Chris Manning. Do you know if she's ill?"

"Let me give you the key," the woman said. "Just drop it in the mailbox when you're through. Say, howzit to Mississippi for me."

She quickly shut her door to the mayhem within.

"I'm sorry not to introduce you," I said. "I don't remember her name. I think she's one of my many second cousins, maybe a Rutledge."

"Quincy Rutledge Perkins," Liz said. "She knows me too."

Chris wasn't home. Kitchen appliances comprised one wall. I placed the box of Chris' office belongings on the unmade Murphy bed. To freshen the heated air in the room, I opened the sliding window but left the shutters closed and locked. The bedroom dresser held a small television.

Liz found a closet next to the door of the bathroom. "No suitcases. Just a few clothes here."

"I'll check the medicine cabinet," I said. The mirror was firmly affixed to the wall, and the free-standing sink and toilet tank were devoid of supplies. "Even though she seemed hassled, Mrs. Perkins retained her dignity," I commented.

Liz rifled through the drawers in Chris' dresser. "Chris didn't intend to leave permanently." Liz held up a photo album. "Family," she said.

I agreed. "A loving family takes precedence." Even in a fire, people grabbed their photographs. "Chris' purse is gone, too."

Liz wrote a note of apology. "Sorry to barge in. Thought you might be ill. Upon your return, please call us."

I signed the sheet of paper, too. "Makes invading her space sound friendlier."

"Will she be re-employed?"

"I'll do my best if, I mean *when* she returns. Remember Halloway seemed to work well with her." I hoped Liz didn't notice that I failed to return Chris' key to the landlady's mail box. The place looked as if Chris would return, but I was paranoid enough to think the entire room could have been staged. I had to admit I read way too many Elizabeth George mysteries. Maybe if Halloway had been an easier person to get along with, less smelly, no doubts or curiosities about the dead and missing women, who had all worked for him, would haunt me.

"Perhaps you should change professions." Liz elbowed me as we drove back to Maui Power. "Apply for an FBI interrogator's job."

Questions of impropriety, misbehavior or worse swirled in my brain. If Pam and Claire hadn't been killed in an accident, would I be thinking more clearly? "Why is Chris not at work?"

"The possibilities are endless," Liz said. "I wonder if the Catholic church has considered that sainthood might be an issue of control."

"You mean I am not concerned, just annoyed that they're no longer under my control?"

"How many bosses get involved in the deaths of their workers?" Liz asked.

Now she had ticked me off. "None," I said. "I don't care what other employers do or think."

I valued these two, went to bat for them, and moved mountains so they could be employed as one person. I wanted them to be able to live the kind of life they envisioned. "It matters to me what happened to them," I said, trying to calm down. They were the first people I hired. "I do not consider employees moveable assets," I added. "They put their trust in me when I hired them." And I for one, meant to keep my end of the bargain.

"Sorry," Liz said, and patted my shoulder. "Too bad we can't ask the police to check the airports."

Maybe I would drive back to Chris' address over the weekend to pound on her neighbors' doors. Ask about strangers.

****

At precisely five o'clock, I tried not to run to my car. As I threw my briefcase onto the passenger seat and turned toward the back of the huge mansion, I realized for the first time that no windows faced landward. My thinking was, no doubt, linked to the fact that I had just completed Elizabeth George's "With No One As Witness." Not many buildings in Maui sported cross ventilation. The ocean provided all the breezes necessary.

In the assigned parking spot next to me, Halloway slammed the door of his maroon Lincoln without saying a polite word. He probably hated seeing the antique 1964 Mustang that Daddy presented me with when I stepped onto Maui's sweet bit of homeland. Halloway seemed greedy enough to sabotage everyone else's enjoyment.

I didn't need the car to appreciate my return to the earth's pinnacle of creation's glory. Halloway's incivility would not lessen my pleasure at being home. Five years of exile for stateside schooling at the sprawling university in Urbana created a yearning for the splendor of Maui and the ocean. Illinois' farmland of distant horizons provided half an hour for tornadoes or dust storms to aim onslaughts of destruction across suddenly insufficient acreage. The sounds, the motion, the brilliant blues, and the turbulence of the sea were wanting in Illinois.

Clear skies shone over Maui, but tension crackled in my body like electrical charges before a storm. Instead of working on next year's personnel projections, I spent an inordinate amount of time filling the scrapbook in my briefcase with accident articles. Reporters failed to answer obvious inconsistencies. What were the reasons for Pam and Claire being in the car? Did they leave their purses in their apartment? What vile creature would rob accident victims?

Halloway didn't seem at all concerned about the accident. Perhaps he couldn't see past the threatening disdain he directed at me. His anger felt aimed at me, like one of those Illinois tornadoes. He was ruining the few accomplishments of my first job. But the next person I hired to sit in front of Halloway's office was going to file a report of his actions every day.

My hand pounded the steering wheel. I wanted that smelly bastard off my back and out of Maui Power's employ. Not that I could fire Halloway; personnel directors held little power. A scapegoat for employee failures more correctly defined my job. The only pleasures came when people I hired thanked me. Striving to lighten the toil of people who needed to earn a decent living, I could shoulder the negative aspects of the job. When first sharing my earnest goal of providing reasons for people to wake up cheerful on a workday, Liz Cameron snickered.

"Saint Svetlana, is it?" she crowed.

When she saw my shocked reaction, she reworded her disdain. "Be nice if someone around here worried about people."

The Cameron family's social status in Maui produced not a flicker of reserve in Liz. She was a senior at Kahului High School when I was a mere sophomore. Even then, I envied her carefree attitude. We kept in touch as sorority sisters of Alpha Emeth. She stayed in Oahu and cautioned me not to attend Urbana. We held in common our homesickness for Maui. I considered Liz my audacious partner rather than my assistant at the power company. She called me a tight ass, to my face. Insubordination be damned, I appreciated her friendship.

I settled for Liz's compliment about my concern for people, but missing and dead secretaries ratcheted up a heavier load than planned when I originally accepted my job. Breathing deeply to calm down, I turned the key in the ignition.

The choice of road home was between Honoapiilani Highway, which ran straight across the island to my home in Wailuku, or the road north. Walls of green from Maui's exotic vegetation on the inland route might calm my jitters, but the northern highway would present oceanic splendor. I headed north but planned to pay attention to the road. I didn't intend to die in a car like Pam and Claire. Thank you, anyway.

My gaze shifted toward the comforting azure ocean, hoping to spot a whale or two off Sugar Beach. Lucky for the whales and bad for me, I didn't see any movement. The polluted bay was Maui Power's responsibility. I cringed whenever I saw the murky waters or heard reports about the utility company's delay in cleaning up the mess. Perhaps politics against polluting the bay contributed to Pam and Claire's decision to work for Maui Power. I hadn't gotten a good night's rest since I heard about the accident. Was I, in any way, responsible?

Another reason I drove north toward Lahaina was that I remembered our cook, Mississippi, commenting about a detective. Her son's friend, a divorce investigator with offices over the Pioneer Inn, was mentioned as the winning variable in a case. Clay Markin. They said he dropped out of the Police Academy. He might possess the contacts I needed to find out more about the accident.

I slowed the Mustang down and pulled into the crowded beach car lot next to the Banyan Tree Park. Instead of heading toward the ocean to gain access to the offices above the Pioneer Inn, I wandered among the tourists on Front Street to sort out my thoughts. None of these people belonged here. I did. I tried to imagine the shoreline sans people, without the buildings. The voices of Lahaina's avid shoppers couldn't drown out the ocean's symphony, but tranquility got lost in the hubbub. Frigid weather on the mainland blossomed tourists under Maui's incessant sun.

Lahaina's Front Street twinkled with Christmas lights. Light posts, even street signs, were festooned with plastic bells and reindeer. The art studios vied with the junk shops for gift dollars. T-shirts, illegal scrimshaw, and imported silk shops; boutiques, leather emporiums; souvenir junk, eel skins, and tattoo parlors outdid each other in garish window decorations inviting prospective Santas to throw away all their money in the twelve days left before Christmas. I blamed my jumpy nerves for my momentary lack of courage. For a further excuse to delay seeking out the investigator's office, I told myself I needed a change of clothing, something that didn't remotely smell like Henry Halloway. I promised myself to return to Front Street on Saturday morning to hire a replacement spy secretary from Clay's agency. Business ethics concerning Halloway's privacy could be set aside, temporarily. Chris Manning needed to be found before another suspicious accident occurred.

Chapter Two

Saturday, December 15

I stepped into Clay Markin's office above the Pioneer Inn, hoping to interest him in the case by presenting myself as a Maui Power Company executive. My tailored linen suit and designer shoes and Coach purse projected elegance. I prayed heaven would bless my first impression.

"I am Svetlana Nigel." I extended my hand. "Personnel Director for the utility company."

"Heard the name." Clay stepped forward, then didn't let go of my hand for a heartbeat or two—a practiced maneuver no doubt, to register his interest.

"Mainland money?" he asked, appraising me slowly from my shoes to the top of my head.

I bowed my head slightly and rolled my blue eyes up as he stood towering over me. The ploy worked on Bogart, not that I remotely resembled Lauren Bacall, or felt the least intimidated. "Once removed niece of Mr. Rutledge. Sugar cane," I explained further, "old money."

"And everything else on Maui." Clay directed me to sit on his leather couch.

I refused to call attention to the grey film of dust covering the soft white leather. The rest of his office was fairly clean, for a man.

Clay claimed a place on the couch. "I didn't think the Rutledge family stooped to hiring detectives."

"Our family's lawyer said you were good." I hoped the made-up compliment meant something to him. Did he see dollar bills piling into the neat corners of his mind?

Clay moved his hand in my direction almost touching my shoulder as if to prove I existed.

I adjusted the side slit of my skirt to cover both knees. "If you can help, I need to find a missing girl and look into a deadly car accident…for the company."

Clay's tone seemed doubtful of my motives. "Why a private detective?"

"The Rutledge family rarely invites public access to our suspicions." I kept my eyes wide open to guarantee I was trustworthy. "You will be the first person to investigate the accident adequately if you get involved."

I watched Clay's mind go into overdrive. "Divorce. I'm a divorce detective."

He might not be of any help, but Clay's concentration and the tension in his body assured me that he didn't want to lose me as a client.

Leaning in my direction, he said. "Demand access to the autopsies to shed light on any discrepancies."

I stared unblinking at Clay Markin.

Male logic wasn't worth the good reputation enjoyed through the ages. I privately failed at an inner pretense of humility. Multiple links between activated parts of my brain spit out silent demands. I could think of a million reasons not to go to the district attorney or the police.

What I wanted, what Pam and Claire needed, and

poor Chris might welcome, was information.

So I said, "If a suspicious accident elicited no response from paid public officials, a missing secretary's plight can just as easily be chalked up to Chris' irresponsibility. My secretary and I went to Chris' apartment...to see if she was ill. Her suitcase, purse, and some belongings were missing."

As I continued to watch him, Clay's muscles rippled and flexed under his thin silk suit, as if his body reacted to a perceived danger.

"Do you work out?" I felt myself blush the moment I asked.

"Why? Do you need someone punched?" His long lashes rose as he watched the blush rise to my hairline.

Then he stared at the floor to give me time to compose myself. As if to further relieve my embarrassment by making himself vulnerable, yet reluctant to share the information, short spurts of words rushed out of his sensuous mouth. "My father was a boxer. First case I solved was where he'd gone. He died on a barroom floor. Downtown Chicago with five aces on the table."

"Do people still do that sort of thing?"

"Dying or gambling?"

"I don't know." I stared at the floor. "The authorities are treating the accident as if there were no questions. I feel responsible for the two secretaries I hired who died last Sunday." I pulled on my curls. "And now their replacement is missing."

"Mayhem on Maui?" Clay's brown eyes focused on the door behind me. "Not likely." But he didn't make a move to dismiss me from the office.

I thought about batting my eyelashes and pulling

out my handkerchief, but couldn't summon the tears necessary to convince him to defend a lady in distress. "If I need to hire another secretary by Monday," I replaced my handkerchief, "would a detective agency be the right place to recruit one?"

"I can't type."

I laughed my best musical, ladylike laugh. Mercy. I hoped I was at least as good at the ploys he'd probably witnessed from a hundred different women. Were the hooks working? Could I trigger his natural masculine impulse to help Chris and find out what really happened to Pam and Claire? I would deal with the guilt of manipulation at a later date. I didn't have much experience in influencing the male gender. Clay reminded me of my dad's old tapes of television reruns where Matt Dillion stepped away from women obviously up to no good. Was Clay as badly used by women as TV episodes implied? Did he believe my quest held any validity? "A female associate or friend that you can trust might help." I refused to leave empty-handed.

"No," Clay said. "There's no one." He watched as I folded my hands prudishly in my lap. He covered them with his big paw and pressed down for a moment on my entwined fingers. Coughing, he straightened his posture, regaining some semblance of order. "Wait, I'll find someone who will do the job," Clay said. "Tell me about the secretaries."

I sank back against the couch. "Where to start? Pam and Claire were killed when their car went off Haleakala Highway at the sixteen-mile marker. The car exploded on impact with the road below."

"Those girls?"

"I knew them well enough to wonder why they were in a car. They both owned bikes and loved to ride up through the clouds to the volcano's crater. Nearly every weekend. Claire said looking down at the rest of the islands made her feel in control."

"Who did the women work for?"

"We worked out a job-sharing arrangement with Maui Power for them. They volunteered so much for the Luckey-Freeland restoration projects that its board granted them honorary membership."

"Hawaiians then?"

"No, but they both felt working on Maui's heritage buildings was part of being a good citizen. 'Saving the jewel,' Pam used to say." Clay waited as I struggled to say more. He wouldn't enjoy witnessing the depth of my frustration. If I got angry enough, I wouldn't be able to stop crying.

"Who did they work for?" he asked, in a non-committal way.

I realized he asked the question twice. "The Purchasing Director, Henry Halloway." His curiosity gave me some hope for a meaningful contribution from him. "And now Chris Manning, their temporary replacement, is missing." I bit a sob of frustration in half. "Will you help?"

Clay looked at his watch.

I admired Clay's compulsion, as an island-bred man, to measure every half-hour of his life. Maybe billing by the hour caused the habit. Was he a man I could trust? I thought about bringing Liz with me to meet Clay but decided against involving her in the investigation. I placed my purse in my lap, resigned to leave graciously if he refused to help.

"A terrible thing." Clay spaced his words between intervals of silence. He lowered his tone as if to ensure I stayed pinned to the couch. "The car nearly fell on a family of tourists. According to the newspaper," he drawled. His leisurely speech irritated me. I was cognizant of the fact that detectives charged by the hour. "...the children saw way too much of the carnage," he said. Clay lapsed into silence, but I felt no urge to leave. Finally, he asked, "Chris Manning worked for Halloway too?"

I tipped my head yes, unsure if my state of stress allowed me to speak without an unprofessional display of additional emotion.

"I have a few contacts in the police department," he offered. "I'll see who I can come up with for a replacement secretary."

"Good." I stood, pleased and then surprised that I was blushing again. "I'll send you a check. How much do you charge?"

"Never mind, your company can afford me." Clay rose from the couch as if reluctant to end the meeting, but the interview was obviously over.

"Yes," I said, stepping closer. "I hope you'll understand, but under the circumstances, I would like the bill sent to my address in Wailuku. It's been a pleasure meeting you."

"Same here." Clay didn't sweep me into his arms as I assumed all divorce detectives did to women within reach. "I'll need your number," he said instead.

I bent over his sandalwood desk, wrote down my address, home, and work numbers. I produced a curt nod and left. When I stepped out of Clay Markin's office onto the Pioneer Inn's second-floor verandah, I took a deep breath, savoring the salty ocean air. Windsurfers hanging from rainbows of parachute sails were tearing up the coastline sky. My heart rushed along with them. Now I'd done it, exposed myself to all sorts of ridicule. Ruminating over the possible sins of Halloway was one thing, but bringing out my fears for public scrutiny left me feeling exposed. Acquaintances complained before about my judgmental attitude.

"Everyone can't be as perfect as you want them," Liz often reminded me.

The gossips on the island would have a field day. The police could even prosecute me for false incrimination of Halloway. Civil courts might sue me and my dad for slander or libel. If the newspapers learned I hired a detective before real evidence came to light, my dad would kill me. I was afraid to admit my job frustrations to Dad, let alone mention my unsubstantiated suspicions about the accident. My professional reputation would be ruined. Psychology courses at Urbana suggested competence-driven personalities tended to denigrate themselves when stressed. So I tried to stop my habit of self-derision by switching my mind to another topic.

Clay Markin was certainly capable-looking. His white silk suit was ostentatious, but I couldn't think of a better outfit to complement his dark complexion. The way he pressed his comforting hand to mine made me wish he'd never stop touching me. The warmth of the leather couch added to the atmosphere of safety. The heat from his interest reached me when I bent over his desk to write down my phone numbers. I didn't need this emotional complication. A biblical phrase or one from Shakespeare rattled through my brain. "Terrible enough was the trouble of the day…" of last week. I shook myself and walked to my car.

At least I had stopped the paranoia about the accident that I seemed to be drowning in. Clay would check out my suspicions. Accidents and missing people, no doubt, fractured the seams of lives less stable than my own. Whether Clay found a spare secretary or more unanswered questions, I was relieved to be able to get on with my life. I looked up at the detective's office from the parking lot. Clay was watching me.

The urge to wave struck, but I restrained myself. What had I gotten myself into? Well aware of my looks, I usually relied on my standoffish attitude to keep men in their place, and off me. But Clay Markin's eyes followed my every move.

Dad accused me of being too proud of my island ancestry to attract a good man. The red hair of the Pele women, who save Maui from volcanoes, kept me noticed enough. Maui society's traditions were a morass of conventions and cautions about acceptable partners and friends. How could pride be an obstacle? If a decent man didn't want a woman who valued who she was, the hell with him.

Clay Markin's male confidence vied with what I hoped was the exposure of emotional vulnerability. He was complicated and unforgettable. Clay might not be as affected as he appeared; success as a divorce detective, prying into the private lives of his clients almost guaranteed a jaded perspective of women. Most of the wives he investigated were no doubt faithful to erring husbands. But now and then he surely found an adventurous huntress who tried out her charms on him.

I had no problem recalling the sultry faces of female students in Urbana. On Maui—probably on all islands—sex needed no artifice. The sun shone less than occurrences of promiscuity. And the sun seldom relented for more than two hours during Maui's long days.

Like gourmet meals, Clay no doubt took every advantage of time and money to pursue the pleasures offered by Maui females. But a steady diet of rich food could lead to indigestion. I planned to take every minute of his time until we figured out what really happened at the accident site and where Chris disappeared. I pulled down the visor of my classic Mustang to inspect my mascara. Vanity was not a pretty emotion, I chastised myself.

I needed to talk to my dad to explain my suspicions about the accident and now Chris. I'd admit I failed to protect the first three people I hired. Dad would call me a bleeding liberal, that the deaths were not my responsibility. But that's not how the trouble felt. Maybe my insecurities made the danger feel personal.

Someone tapped on the passenger's window.

Clay.

Had he seen me preening?

Clay came around to my side of the car. I rolled down my window.

"Classy car," Clay said.

I took the key out of the ignition. "Did I forget anything?"

"Would you like to grab a bite, maybe a drink?" He smiled his slow easy smile, a bit too welcoming for my taste. "Before you drive back to Wailuku?"

"Well, I might," I said, trying not to jump out of

the car. Nothing to do at home, anyway.

Clay offered his hand to help me out of the car. I had already slammed and locked the Mustang's door before I noticed his proffered aid. "If I'm not lounging around in Hana," Clay took my arm as we walked back to the Inn, "I live upstairs behind my office."

Oh, oh. I was warned by my speeding heart.

"The bar downstairs serves great gumbo."

"That's good," I said, relieved at the invitation.

"You can meet an old girl…." He stopped talking and I knew the word 'friend' failed to clear his throat. Clay continued. "I dropped out of the Police Academy when I was twenty-two. Before I started the 'Information Agency.'" He laughed at a joke I missed. "I'm trying to tell you about Gail Maynard."

He opened the bar's screen door and let me enter first. "Gail didn't finish the academy, either, and I'm pretty sure she'd jump at the chance to get involved in one of my cases."

My eyes adjusted to the sudden gloom. Half of the bulbs in a string of Christmas lights over the bar were out. The dark red counter and matching Formica tables subdued any reflections from the windows facing the brilliant ocean. Dark paneling added to the sense of cool relief from the pelting sunshine.

At a table near the door, one unspeaking married couple eyed each other without interest. Tourists, I labeled them when I noticed their identical cameras. Competitive in all, I surmised.

The bar customers commanded more attention than the drab tourist couple. A few patrons lolled at the bar: the bartender, two men, and one woman in a sixties get-up, faded skirt, and matching beads. The man in a policeman's uniform was larger than Clay's six-foot, five inches.

"Gail," Clay called to the back of the gray-haired woman whose long thick locks touched the bar stool rim. Clay pointed to me. "I found a job for you."

Gail finished her oily brown drink before slurring. "I don't do housework, even for myself." Her laughter contained a certain naughtiness.

My grade-school nuns rapped knuckles with a ruler for less in decorum.

"Run up my tab, Luckey." Clay motioned for Gail to get off her stool and join us at a nearly clean table.

"Jim Luckey?" I asked.

"That's me," he said.

"You knew the girls who were killed in that accident last Sunday."

"Worked for the restoration project. No slackers, those two."

Luckey started to sit down at the table, before remembering his duties as a bartender. "Sorry, what would you like?"

"Same ol' Bud," Clay said. "Bring Gail a cup of coffee and a Kaluha and cream."

"Two," Gail said. "I don't want you to feel pressured if you get busy." Gail giggled. "Nothing like a wide-awake drunk."

Fumes of brandy permeated the air around her. She tied the ends of the ragged hem of her dress into a knot in her lap. Her bare legs showed unshaven black hairs. I thought I heard an Australian accent from the woman, but couldn't pin it down.

Luckey hadn't moved, and I realized I should ask for alcohol. "Perhaps Cream Sherry," I said and watched him wink at Clay.

"Rutledge family," Clay explained to his buddies. "And three bowls of gumbo." He patted Gail's head.

"Second cousin to them," I stumbled over my embarrassment. Then I blurted out, "My dead mother's relatives."

At that revelation, Clay stared at me. But Gail started blubbering. At first, I thought she was choking from lack of liquor, but she escalated into a fountain of grief with a slight cough interrupting her sporadic wails. Apparently, alcohol intensified a wide range of emotions.

Luckey brought our order. The big cop at the bar came with him and then glared down at me.

"It's okay, Bear," Clay explained. "Svetlana mentioned her mother's death."

"Mississippi's Bear?" I asked.

The giant nodded but didn't move back to the bar until I patted Gail's sticky hand. "There, there. I was only five," I explained as solace for them.

Clay coughed. "Miss Nigel thinks last Sunday's accident should be investigated."

"She's right," Luckey said, ignoring Gail's hiccups. "Pam and Claire wouldn't use a car."

Gail quit her display of weeping as quickly as she started the flood. She wiped her face with her hair, which nearly caused me to jump away from the table. Gail swallowed the contents of her newly arrived drink before taking a slight sip of coffee. She frowned at the caffeine's sobering effect. "Is this a new case for ya then, Clay?"

Clay admitted as much and Gail straightened, rebuttoning a low button on her dingy blouse. "You'll

need to cancel our reservations for next week in Hana."
Gail bobbed her head in my direction to emphasize the
hint of a pre-existing relationship. "Since the man loves
sunsets better than sunrises, I suppose you'll be needing
my help on the job?"

"Yes," I said, not really meaning it. I wouldn't hire
the woman to cut grass, certainly not for a secretarial
job.

"I'll clean up," Gail said, marking my doubtful
tone.

Luckey hadn't strayed far from our table. "Tanner
probably autopsied the girls."

"You should meet our old teacher," Gail said.
"Believe it or not, Captain Tanner will give me a good
recommendation. Clay and I jumped ship at the same
time."

I tried to ignore the implication that Gail and Clay
were involved in more than learning police tactics. She
was ten years Clay's senior, and Clay had at least ten
years on me. "Could you fill in as a secretary?" I turned
to Jim Luckey to explain. "The secretary that I hired to
replace Pam and Claire is missing."

"God," Gail said, elongating the word enough for
the Trinity to claim.

"You only need to keep your eyes open." Clay
tried to alleviate any fears Gail might entertain against
taking the job.

"And make copies of everything you can find," I
added.

"At a secretary's hourly rate?" Gail asked.

"Big retainer up front." Clay motioned toward my
purse.

"Oh, right," I said. I didn't know how much cash I

carried.

I counted out ten fifties before Clay said, "Fine."

"Damn straight," Gail pocketed the entire sum. She bowed to us from her seated position. "Where's the job?"

"Maui Power, Monday?" Clay asked me.

I agreed. "First floor, Personnel Office. To the right of the front door. You will see the sign." The case was already out of my hands.

"Don't forget to explain to my new boss that I'm a spiritualist," Gail called to us on her unsteady trip back to the bar. "Criminals are doomed to inherit past evil lives."

Luckey went back to the bar to fill Gail's empty glass. Somewhat stunned, I watched Gail resume her seat at the bar, empty glass thrust toward the bartender. Then I sighed when I realized my omission of a retainer. "Sorry, Clay. I'll write you a check. Would a thousand dollars help?"

"Absolutely," Clay said, not bashful about watching me write out the sum.

"Don't forget that old tab," Luckey laughed. "Divorce detectives spend more than they conjure up by ruining other people's lives."

Clay's chin went up in his own defense. "Facts prove husbands don't feel loved. Even when their wives fail to partake in illicit activities. Women know how to attract men." He waved his hand in the direction of my slit skirt. "Not how to love them. Not that it matters."

The explanation of his single status mattered to me. God alone understood why.

"Coffee," Clay called.

I shifted my gaze to the couple near the door. Their

31

food was gone but not a word released from their tightened mouths.

"Known Gail for over ten years." Clay lowered his voice as he explained the relationship. "First met her intoxicated and well-used in my apartment upstairs. I took her to the hospital and answered all their questions about abuse. They suspected me. Even above her denials and with Luckey giving me an alibi. Gail couldn't remember who hurt her. Frequent blackouts and her propensity to lie caused us both to be expelled from the Police Academy. The worst part is she wastes so much time. Hours of her life poured down the drain."

"Will Tanner recommend Gail?" I kept my eyes lowered not to reveal how shocking I found this news bit.

"She needs the work," Clay said. "I attended AA meetings with her. Then Alanon. She needs a reason to stop. I thought I was to blame."

I watched him glance in Gail's direction. She seemed permanently encamped at the end of the bar. He was a nice guy, trying to rehabilitate a friend. I gave him my best smile and didn't hesitate to touch the wrist of his giant hand spread palm up on the table.

He gently squeezed my hand, continuing to clarify Gail's comments about Hana. "When making money by the hour gets to me, I rent a place in Hana. Rooms are perched in the branches of five kukui-nut trees. Not even the rain ruins the sense of arriving a minute after creation." Clay moved closer as if to plumb the depths of my soul with his searching eyes. My breath caught in my throat as I relaxed into the low tenor of his continuing description.

"When I face the Pacific," he said, "with the hills

of Mauna Kea poking through the clouds, all things seem possible. Aromas of flowers and fruit seep into my lungs. I run along the black beaches an hour before the tourists start gawking."

I gazed at his toned body and imagined him striding the red sand shoreline of the nude beach in Hana. I exhaled awe. Flecks of sunshine sparkled around him.

"Pounding water lets me reclaim my world," Clay ended his soliloquy.

"Our Maui," I added, not caring if I appeared smitten by his words.

"Lazy days summon up the disparity between my goal of living in beauty and my present choice of careers."

"A poet. Yes, you are." A fleeting thought stopped right between my eyes. This could be the one, the man I might love for the rest of my life. I shook my head to stay on track. "If Tanner gives Gail a recommendation, I'll hire her," I said. I admired the charm of Clay's warm smile. His nostrils flared as he inhaled my perfume. "I won't starve," I added, "but my job is on the line."

Clay was, no doubt, irresistible when he was twenty-two. After all the warnings from my father and Mississippi, I knew I might enjoy getting emotionally involved with this unsuitable chap. Were doors opening toward a world I hadn't had time to explore? When I pulled myself away from drinking two more glasses of sherry, eating a bowl of too spicy gumbo and Clay's company, I drove back to Wailuku.

A yellow pick-up followed me past the block-wide banyan tree next to the Pioneer Inn. The truck's bent

and rusted fender stayed in my rear-view mirror all the
way home.

Chapter Three

Sunday, December 16

Liz was right: I could detect as well as the next person. That was my first awake thought. The night before Clay said he would call the police station with a description of the yellow pick-up that followed me home. How many yellow pick-ups could there be on Maui? I didn't hold out much hope for the police. So far, they failed to trace down the owner of the car that Pam and Claire died in.

Monday morning I would search through the application files from all three women. I doubted they shared more in common than the secretarial position under Henry Halloway.

I focused on the new day outside my bedroom windows. The sun refused to shine on Sunday, its name's day. Instead, rain fell from a thick gray sky. I fluffed my pillows, turned on the light switch next to my bedside table, and leaned back on my pillows to ease into the day.

The ceiling fan and lights caused the coral-rose walls to pulsate reflections into the glowing mirrored wall of closets facing my bed. New worlds were opening all around me. I raised my hand to stare at the remembered brief touch of Clay's. A universe of sensations and yearnings awaited. But I didn't have time to explore them. The lives of three women haunted my thoughts. A late bloomer, that's what people called me.

On the mainland, my emotions were kept in check. I lived a year in the brick, turreted Alpha Emeth house in Urbana. Dad suggested I make those in charge of Urbana invitations aware of the fact that my mother had been a member of Alpha Emeth when she was at Pacific University. The rounded stained-glass windows in the sorority dining room created an ethereal pleasantness. The dances in the ballroom upstairs with matching bay windows were equally fine.

Two years before I joined, Liz Cameron was invited to the Oahu-based house of the sorority. When Liz graduated and went to work for Maui Power, our fun of comparing notes about the saccharine rituals and publicity-minded charity work ended.

The time I spent chatting with my constantly changing roommates, besides the added hours wasted in social functions, I thought, warranted my leaving the residence. I wanted to concentrate on my studies and return home to Maui as quickly as possible.

I did not redecorate the private university dorm room. I lived in seclusion with the steel cots, the musty carpet, and dusty drapes. I forced myself to focus on my studies. Earphones and my Hawaiian CDs helped drown the surrounding clamor. I wasn't going to fail because of homesickness or invitations from female or male acquaintances. The warm spring nights after the blustery winters were the hardest to ignore.

My holidays in Maui held out the promise of the life I would someday be privileged to share, if I stayed on track. I kept my heart reined in to let my brain suck up every bit of knowledge offered at the university. I did not want anyone to claim my future accomplishments could be chalked up to my family's finances and influence. I intended to be of value and service, to earn my own place in the world.

Henry Halloway's yellow smirk of disdain flashed before me. I understood his view of my position at Maui Power for half a second. Then, increasing traffic noises seeped through the lush tropical foliage surrounding my father's home. Mill Street was the center of Wailuku's happy valley, a verdant swath. Loud mynah birds made their sunrise cries. The pelting rain on the palm trees, elephant ear taro, and ironwood trees added noisy resistance to the wind.

Even though I appreciated being home, I didn't plan to live with Mississippi and Kani a day longer than needed. I couldn't afford a comparable place on my salary. I blamed my mainland living experience for negative ideas about renting the type of sterile apartment I could afford on Maui and doing without the convenience of Father's live-in cook.

I noticed that since I met Clay, I ceased to think of Kani Nigel as Daddy or Dad. The term father seemed to mark a transition in my thinking. Probably some deep psychological meaning was attached to switching allegiances to another alpha male in my life.

Meanwhile, the Nigel acreage ceased to be one of the quietest places in Wailuku. I held my pillows against my ears. Construction noises behind the Mission House down the street prevented any further rest. Sundays guaranteed no mercy. The workers probably appreciated the overtime and some deadline of financing or grant money, no doubt, spurred the unholy activity.

I struggled to be released from the restraining covers and then headed for the bathroom. My brain refused to coast as I attended to the morning's ministrations.

Apparently, most restoration projects like the Bailey Mission Museum and the Pioneer Inn ended up in their original colors, green and white. Reconstructing history held certain decorating drawbacks. I thought coral rose would stand out better against the green vegetation when seen from the bay or the ocean.

I wondered what colors my mother, Karen, liked. I knew I could not ask Mississippi without risking her tears. Mississippi and my father usually ended conversations about my mother in a snit, followed by weeks of cold silences. I racked my brain for ways to steer clear of the repetitive performances, usually choosing avoidance. Questioning either of them in private garnered short answers and long, grief-riled periods of silence.

As I dressed for brunch, my brain pursued fifteen different subjects: from what colors Clay liked best to how I was going to pass Gail off as a secretary to Halloway, and if there was still time to attend St. Andrew's service. The priority to be resolved at breakfast was informing my father about Clay. I could calmly bring up the case and let my enthusiasm for Clay reveal itself. First, I would mention the accident. I retrieved the finished scrapbook from my briefcase. The pages were filled with news articles about the crash.

Kani would acknowledge the freak accident deserved at least my scrutiny. Of course, Father would understand that I wanted to know all the details of Pam and Claire's demise. Then I could mention that I used Mississippi's recommendation for a detective. The mystery of Chris Manning's whereabouts would add to the reasonableness of hiring someone as a spy in the position they each had held. That ought to convince him.

I discovered why it was raining. Mississippi captured the sun by filling our long dining room table with heaps of colorful flowers. The sky was weeping at their loss.

"Good to see you could make it, Sunny," Kani said, tipping his cheek for a kiss as he folded the morning's Hawaiian Gazette.

At fifteen I remembered declining because I thought the greeting a snide remark about my late rising. Which, no doubt it was; but I kissed my father's cheek under Mississippi's watchful eye. I was glad to be home but kept the thought of moving on when the time was right.

Mississippi shrugged and handed me a steaming plate: scrambled eggs, cornbread, honey, and pineapple. More particles from the captured sun lay in broken yellow pieces on my plate.

Ignoring the food, I launched into a lengthy defense of my developing friendship with a detective. The protection of secretaries I hired suffered in the translation. The scrapbook of accident articles remained on the floor next to my chair, forgotten in my fresh enthusiasm for Clay's abilities. The more I talked about him, the better he seemed. The subject ended with three long moments of silence.

"Svetlana, I know that child's mother," Mississippi said, as she poured Kani more coffee.

"Karen's best friend." Kani's tone was quarrelsome.

"Didn't say she wasn't." Now Mississippi showed hurt feelings. "Tennessee Huggins Markin and your Karen Rutledge were sisters to the bone, even if they shared no blood."

I trained myself to keep my head down during these outbursts, which occurred without fail after my mother's name was mentioned. Somehow, both their wounds and grief, stayed as fresh and vibrant as the flowers gracing the table.

Mississippi dropped an emptied serving plate behind Father's chair. He jumped at the noise but didn't offer to help pick up the pieces. I saw Mississippi kick a few pieces under the table. She was determined to have her say this time. "The Sojourns are the fourth generation connection. My son, Bear, and Tennessee's Clay stayed friends even after the Academy. We Huggins were cousins to that Maui side of the Rutledge family, long before Clay's father came on shore."

"The slacker," Kani nearly spat.

"Clay solved his first case for his mother," I intervened, hoping for peace. "He discovered where his father ended up."

Then I realized I was babbling. They already knew about Chicago's barroom floor with five aces on the table. At least they both liked Tennessee, and I didn't have to argue about Clay's acceptable social standing.

"Tennessee lives just down the road in Kahului," Mississippi offered me.

Kani glared at her. "Lot of good that does."

Mississippi ignored his sour grapes. "Your mother had that house built for Tennessee Huggins."

"Why was that?" I asked, feeling brave about continuing the conversation.

"Tennessee was the real estate agent that found this home for us," Father's voice nearly faltered with emotion.

Mississippi changed the subject abruptly as if in sympathy. "Bear will be bringing the tree down this morning. Not that long till Christmas."

"Svetlana, you could find all the information you want on your own." Kani stopped in the doorway to his study. "Any reason for me to worry about you?"

"Clay says the pick-up that followed me last night will be easy to find on Maui."

Kani looked at Mississippi, then me. I no longer felt he discounted my revelations as a schoolgirl's emotional infatuation. Worry etched a line between his eyebrows.

As if to explain, he called to us as he left the house, "I'm walking down to Tennessee's. Call her and warn her I'm coming."

"Why does Clay's mother need a warning?" I asked.

"Never mind, honey," Mississippi said. "You got enough to fill your worrying head today."

What I didn't need from Mississippi, but loved her too much to complain, was being treated like a child. If I wasn't still living at home, Mississippi would have no cause to speak down to me. At least Father called me Svetlana as if to recognize the new responsibility I was undertaking to discover what happened to the three secretaries.

****

Early that afternoon, Clay Markin called the house.

"Tanner's working today. You should meet him. Get a recommendation for Gail Maynard. For Halloway's secretarial spying."

"Certainly. I'll be ready in ten minutes," I said, trying not to purr. My excitement couldn't be assigned to the case. I was actually looking forward to seeing Clay Markin again.

When I tried to open the front door and run down the steps to climb into his MG, Mississippi barred the way. "Just you wait till he comes to the door."

"Mississippi!" I stomped my foot, acting the part of the child she thought I was.

The door burst open from Mississippi's pulling and Clay's pushing as I nearly shouted my best defense against propriety. "It's not like I'm a virgin anymore."

The three of us stood there looking at each other.

"Well obviously, you could still learn a few manners." Mississippi stomped off.

Clay tried to ignore my embarrassment. "Let's move on, shall we? The rain stopped."

"Yes," I said. Damn. Oh well, the information exchange was perhaps meant to be. God help us all. "Wahikuli Park?"

Clay opened my door and I folded myself into the car. "The Civic Center, Medical Center and Morgue are on Prison Street," he said.

"This is my first visit," I said, wishing I could switch from this teenage personality into the woman I really was. I repeated the Hawaiian names out loud to relax my voice, "Between Hahaione and Haanapali.

"Can't avoid the place." Clay gunned the car to cleave to the winding road. "Now that you've decided to save the world."

"The truth will do," I said.

****

Across the road from the Police Station in Wahikuli, the setting sun pounded the beach of Wayside Park. The volcanic gravel parking lot off Prison Street gave a somber aspect to the civic center. Red hibiscuses bloomed above the croton hedges lining the narrow lawn. Their fragrances added to the soft trade winds blowing the leaves of the giant Koa tree up the hill, inland. Comparing the scene to Clay's office view, I could understand why Clay might have continued as a trainee if the station had faced the ocean.

Inside the building, Clay called to an older man, "Captain Tanner."

The captain, who stood in the only office with a door, measured half the size of Clay. Tanner waved at us to join him in the windowless office.

As we passed two younger officers, they said, "Howzit." Clay acknowledged and returned their greetings. I marked the proof of Clay's constant contact with the department. Good news for the investigation. As I turned to nod hello too, my heel caught on a computer wire. Clay deftly steadied me with his hand on my waist and explained to the audience. "First time in a police station."

They nodded and I pulled on my curls.

To Tanner, the initial words out of Clay's mouth were, "Employed by the Rutledges." I could see Clay wanted that cleared up first. "…on that car crash off Haleakala Highway."

"Let me introduce myself," I said, not believing a smile was appropriate under the circumstances. "Svetlana Nigel."

"Impressive clients." Tanner lit a cigarette pulled from above his ear, then immediately put it out. "What's your connection to the girls?"

"I think I'll wait on that." Clay held the cards he didn't have closer to his chest. "Any theories on the accident?"

Tanner picked up a pack of cigarettes out of his top desk drawer. "You know, Miss, Clay is a divorce investigator, not a criminal detective." I indicated that I understood the distinction by nodding soberly. "We went by the book," Tanner said. "When no alcohol or drugs were found, we sent the bodies back to their mainland families."

I could see Clay knew the captain hated rules. And, I knew the man's professional life depended on following all the rules: dotting every 'i', crossing every 't'. "Did Penelope Windgate baby-sit the bodies?" Clay asked.

Tanner cheered up slightly. "She's the medical examiner," he told me.

"Fussy old maid," Clay added. "She probably made a few extra observations before the bodies were shipped home." Tanner nodded in agreement. Clay opened the door of the small office. "I'll make sure you get a copy of any notes."

Tanner banged him on the back. "Know I can count on you."

"We almost forgot." It was a good thing Tanner shook Clay's thought loose. "We need clearance to go through the apartments of three women. Chris Manning, a temporary replacement for the other two secretaries, is missing."

"Give me their addresses." Tanner handed me a

legal pad.

I wrote down the address near Hana for Chris and the one in Olowlau for Pam and Claire.

"You said you would run a check on that yellow pick-up." Clay looked in my direction and I knew he telegraphed concern for me to Tanner.

"No problem," Tanner said. "I can get search warrants for all three of the girls' apartments by five Monday."

"You only need two," I said. "Claire and Pam lived together."

Clay checked his watch, for billing purposes. "Cease the hour," he said. "We'll be back tomorrow."

"I'll send Bear Huggins with you," Captain Tanner said. "Make it more legal."

"What about Gail Maynard and the yellow truck?" I asked.

"Who?" Tanner asked.

"The old dame in my criminal justice class." Clay was irritated at the captain's temporary lapse of memory.

"You mean the Nigel family," Tanner winked at me, "not the Rutledges, don't you?"

"Yeah, yeah. Svetlana is the personnel director out at Maui Power. The dead women and the missing woman all worked for the purchasing manager, Henry Halloway. Gail needs a recommendation from you to be hired as an undercover secretary for Halloway, the manager. Remember Gail, lots of hair, wore skirts that dragged on the floor? Gave you a hell of a time."

Not much to recommend a detective, I thought.

"You're the only one that gave me trouble in that class. Wait, discretion. She wanted a definition for police discretion in the use of force."

"That's Gail," Clay said cheerfully to me.

"She dropped out," Tanner said. "What's her name?"

"Gail, Gail Maynard." Clay clenched his fist in frustration.

Captain Tanner shook his head, then rummaged around in a dusty file cabinet in the corner. "Class lists," he explained to me. "Here she is, always late. Lives in Hana. We investigated her once for fraud. Tells fortunes but doesn't accept money, so we couldn't charge her. Upsets people something fierce."

"Captain," Clay started, lapsing into the refuge of politeness

"Call me Tanner."

Clay continued, controlling his tone with difficulty by staring at his watch. "Call Gail, explain you gave her a good recommendation."

"Are you sure?" Tanner asked me. "This woman doesn't know when to shut up."

Clay backed out of the office door, tugging on my purse.

I could only pray that Gail had learned enough about police work to handle the job of spying on Halloway by herself. I didn't budge from Tanner's office. "And the yellow pick-up?" I asked.

"Need the license number," Tanner said to Clay.

Chapter Four

I hoped Clay would agree to witness Gail's first meeting with Halloway. "I could pick you up on the way to work," I said.

"Might as well show up to ruffle Halloway's feathers?" Clay asked.

"Maybe you could tell Halloway that the police asked you to look into the missing person report of Chris Manning." I wanted to see Clay, hear his voice, claim his time for myself.

"Are you worried Halloway won't accept Gail?" Clay opened the door of his MG.

"Yes," I admitted, hoping that would motivate him to accompany me. On the ride back to my house, Clay kept his own counsel. I wondered if I was on the clock. Would he charge me for the ride home?

Mississippi was pruning her roses along the front steps when we drove up. A suspiciously convenient timing of the task I thought as we walked up the steps to the entrance.

"See you soon," Clay and I said at the same time. I was moved by the coincidence of words. Actually, I didn't believe in chance circumstances. The earth moved with reason, the ocean knew its destiny. I went to my room wondering if I could name the warm glow I was experiencing. Could be wonder. Or hope.

****

Monday, December 17

The next morning, Clay stood in the parking lot of Pioneer Inn as I drove up. His body looked tense. He leaned down stiffly to speak. I smiled, surprised at how comfortable I felt around a stranger I had only met on Saturday. I motioned for him to get in the car. My secretary, Liz, would be proud of me for being so adventurous with an eligible man.

Clay appeared glad to see me. Maybe he was relieved to see me alive, in person. He smiled without restraint as he opened the passenger door.

"Good news?" I asked, thinking his response showed his mood.

Clay put his hand on his forehead, and forced himself to frown. My window was open and I hoped my perfume floated to his side of the car. "Do you mind driving a little out of the way?" he said as if needing to pull himself together. Clay reached for index cards inside his coat. They were filled with notes, probably about the accidents. His fingers brushed the white silk of his suit coat.

I reached over and patted his knee to get his attention. "Ready?"

Clay jumped as if I'd slapped him. "Up Front Street." He deepened his voice, "Then the road inland."

I followed his directions. "We need to be at Maui Power before Gail arrives." No comment. "Did I upset you when I touched you?"

"Of course," he said, giving me a slow, full-wattage smile. "My client is the most beautiful woman on Maui." He tried to turn around to look out the back window. The Mustang was too small for that maneuver, so he tilted the rear-view mirror in his direction.

48

I concentrated on the road. I wanted to test out my responses to the man whose massive frame filled the car. Clay Markin certainly knew how to shower one with compliments. But he did seem moved when he first saw me. Maybe I misunderstood his emotions. Maybe the horrors he imagined involving the secretaries created the tension I felt when my hand touched his knee. His smile made it difficult to think about driving. One thing I knew for certain, we could *not* end up at Maui Power driving in this direction. "Where are we going?"

"Pull off here." Clay indicated a steep dirt side road. "The truck I called Tanner about followed you into Lahiana."

The Mustang didn't sport air conditioning which might explain my freezing hands, but I admitted to myself that cold fear was the culprit. "Did you get his license number?"

"I already phoned the plate number into Tanner, H802." He patted his chest where I imagined his cell phone resided. "Give me your cell phone number."

"Did we give the pick-up the slip?"

"The driver knows where you're headed this morning. I just wanted to talk to you for a minute." I gave him my cell phone number for the second time. "You are in danger." Clay wrote the digits on a blank index card. "And, I need to speak to your father."

I nervously tapped the steering wheel. "Is there any news from Tanner about Chris Manning?" I didn't expect good news.

"Tanner's checking the airport in Hana and Kapalua for outgoing flights." Clay straightened his coat jacket.

I wanted all the warm white silk of the man around me, protecting me in his safe arms. "What did Tanner think of your threatening Halloway?" I didn't want the statement to sound like a question, but my emotions tended to raise my voice an octave.

He grinned at me, delighted with his role of the protective male. "Tanner agreed. Thought I could get some leads." Clay unfolded himself from the car and came around to the driver's side.

I opened the door. My knees felt weak as I slipped my hand into his and stepped out of the car.

"I'll drive down to Kihei." Clay didn't step away from me.

The warmth of the man seeped into my pores. My brain went on standby. "I live up-wind in Wailuku." Without hesitation, I gave him my keys. "But I love this side. The hills are nearer the ocean here." I stammered, "...bet, better views from the roads." His huge hand continued to hold mine and the keys. If I talked non-stop, maybe my body would get a grip. "Pam and Claire shared an apartment in Olowalu."

"Short bike ride to their job. You told me." Clay released my hand. "After you left last night, I couldn't stop thinking of you."

"Above the general store," I added. "...that's where the girls lived."

"I even dreamed about looking for your red curls among some," he coughed and I knew he withheld prurient details, "bathing beauties in Hana." Clay turned lazily toward the preeminent ocean. "My nightmares repeat themselves."

"Searching for me was a nightmare?"

I heard his laugh rumble in his chest before it burst

forth, scaring a flock of sparrows in the roadside grasses. "No, no." His sudden stillness alerted my senses to the size of the man standing next to me. The top of my head didn't reach the knot in his white tie. A gentleness, even a sadness, drew me to him. "The familiar sound effects of last night's high surf," Clay's voice drifted into a soft melancholy as if the dreamscape of the night before had settled on him, "from a storm on the equator slashing against the pier outside the Inn. Triggers the same dream."

His head tipped in my direction as if to acknowledge that I stood there listening intently. "I wake up in the dream; I guess I'm about five, calling to my mother that the storm is knocking."

"Hugs keep away the storm," I said, repeating Mississippi's comfort.

"Mother's words exactly." Clay shivered as if the covers needed to be pulled up. "I always follow that dream with a sequel nightmare." We made eye contact and I waited. "I'll tell you about it when I know you better," he said.

"You better." I laughed trying to shift his mood.

"Did you go to Chris Manning's apartment to check on her again?" Clay asked.

It took me a minute to realize what he was asking. "Yes, no. Liz, my secretary, and I returned a box of Chris' belongings. I meant to go back to talk to the neighbors before I hired Gail."

Clay moved closer to me as I leaned against the car. His hip was nearly touching mine as we took in the view as if we had dismissed all obligations to time. My tension followed the multi-colored parachutes of the sky-skiers lazily trailing their boats. The dock and Front

Street were hidden, with only a few rooftops peeking above the trees. From the hill's vantage point, all was ocean, peaceful.

"Can Gail be any good as a spy?" I tugged at the back of my curls, not meaning to be critical of his decision or dispute his abilities or even demean his background. I turned to apologize to him, reaching up to place my hand on his shoulder. "Well, I know you're the best."

He laid his large hand on mine, and I received the same assurance of warmth from his hand as I remembered from his touch when we first met. Our mutual silence confirmed the formation of a fledgling bond.

He did say he wanted to talk to my father. Of course, he meant to talk about the pick-up truck following me. The conversation surely wouldn't include anything of a personal nature.

As if reading my mind, Clay leaned down and kissed my mouth for a brief minute. "Svetlana, I want to get more involved with you." Clay let go of my warmed fingertips and turned toward the coastline. "But we need to focus."

"Yes," I stammered, taken by surprise by his words and kiss. My whispered response implied that I, too, was holding back. "This case is serious business."

Clay walked me to the passenger side of the car, an arm around my shoulder. "I asked Tanner to get a search warrant of Halloway's home and the utility company from the District Attorney, but he needs more evidence before he'll submit the request."

"Then Gail will have to work out as a spy."

On the drive south, past the beaches of Olowalu,

Ma'alaea Bay was still dark and muddy from the utility plant's debris and garbage spills. My heart leaped in my throat when I saw a whale surface at the mouth of the bay.

****

When we arrived at Maui Power, I could tell that Liz spent her entire weekend decorating the front foyer. Two huge trees flocked in white snow stood on each side of the circular staircase. The trees were decorated with blue lights in the shape of stars. Twirling blue icicles seemed to emit a constant chime. White poinsettias competed for attention with banks of presents wrapped in blue tinfoil. I shuddered to think about my January Master Card bill.

Gail Maynard was waiting in Liz's outer office, which continued the theme of blue and white decorations. An entirely white and gold Saint Nicholas dominated her desk area.

"I notice your elevators are only used by the disabled," Gail complained without bothering to stand up.

Liz gave me a questioning look.

I knew why. Gail's attempt at dressing professionally failed miserably.

"Just give Clay and me a moment, Gail." To Liz, I directed, "If you would take Gail over to the Benefits Office, she can fill out our application in their office." In order to clearly communicate my decision, I added, "Gail will be working for Mr. Halloway." Then I explained Clay's presence to Liz, "Clay Markin is a friend of my father's."

"No," Gail and Liz both disputed my cover story.

"He's a divorce detective," Liz said. "And your

father is a widower."

"The police hired me to look into Chris Manning's disappearance," Clay said.

"I can buy that," Liz said, smiling at me.

"Is there anything left on Maui of Christmas decorations?" I complimented her endeavors.

"Nothing blue or white." She winked at me and handed back my credit card.

"The police didn't ask you to check on Chris Manning though, did they?" Gail's irritating way of speaking to Clay grated on my nerves.

"Nevertheless," I said as forcefully as I could to put an end to further discussion. I ushered Clay into my office, which looked slightly askew. The chairs were repositioned, incorrectly. "Maybe a new cleaning lady?" I motioned for Clay to take a seat on my couch.

"Or your secretary's efforts at decoration," he said.

The philodendron on my filing cabinet was pushed all the way to the mirror, but nearly two dozen Christmas balls were spiked into the soil of the plant. I pulled off some of the damaged leaves that were crushed between the wall and the files. On the wall behind my desk, the horizontal mirror on top of the file cabinets faced the door. I didn't know all the principles of Feng Shui flow, but I grasped the fact that people straightened up in front of mirrors. Usually, visitors would adjust their faces to smile at themselves. Even complainers changed the tone of negative scripts in the light of their own reflected smiles. The middle desk drawer stuck as I tried to pull out my calendar. "Someone has searched my office. They've gone through everything."

"Your secretary must have seen them," Clay said.

I wiped a frown from my face when Halloway suddenly pushed open my office door.

"Got a moment?"

"Sure." I swallowed hard, trying not to take in any of the tainted oxygen that surrounded Halloway. "Have you had your coffee yet?"

"Yes. Haven't you?"

Don't get panicky, I told myself and introduced Clay. "This is Detective Clay Markin."

I got up and leisurely walked out to Liz's office to make coffee. I replenished my lungs with clean air in Liz's office. Then, I returned at a purposely decelerated pace, giving the men time to size each other up. "How can I help you this morning, Mr. Halloway?" I asked, trying to only exhale.

"Chris has not returned."

"Your temporary help is filling out forms in Liz's office." I sat behind my desk and waited for Halloway to re-adjust his demeanor in the mirror behind me.

Instead, he glared down at me. "Let's just end Chris Manning's employment." Halloway finally sat in a chair on the opposite side of my glass-topped desk. As an obvious afterthought, he smiled back at Clay. Halloway's tan teeth almost complimented his yellowing skin.

"We can do that," I said. The aroma of coffee from Liz's office didn't help to settle my nervous stomach but it did mask Halloway's offensive odor.

"I hope you found me a steady person this time." Halloway rose to leave and turned toward Clay. "Are you helping in the quest for a competent secretary?"

"Maybe." Clay's vaguely threatening tone hung in the air.

I hated Halloway's arrogance with all my heart. "I think you will find Gail Maynard a steady, devoted assistant. We'll bring her up shortly."

"Good," he said as he left.

Coffee? I didn't need any other stimulant for the day, but I wheeled in Liz's cart and poured Clay and myself each a cup. Holding the comforting warmth of the cup, an involuntary shudder escaped me. "Offering virgins to a jealous, vengeful God, I am." Clay listened patiently to my rantings. "First Pam and Claire, sweet, helpful women. Maybe they were a bit high-and-mighty, deciding what people should think and how they should save the planet."

"I don't think I ever saw them on the island." Clay finished his cup and bent down to place it on the bottom rack of the cart. "I'm curious if either young woman found out something about Halloway that he didn't want broadcast...besides that odor."

"Claire's black hair didn't cover her large ears." Senseless non-sequiturs sprouted from my mouth as my brain busily mulled over the possibilities of corruption in a purchasing office. "Pam's blonde tresses were swept back in a severe twist. Curls escaped near her brow and ears."

"Maybe they discovered an illegal purchasing scheme?" Clay asked.

I sat mute behind my desk. The coffee was chilled by the time I took my first sip. "And Chris Manning, a more cheerful person you couldn't ask for. A little overweight, but everyone loved her."

"How could she raise Halloway's ire?" Clay mused. I loved the low timbre of his voice. My nerves welcomed the resonance. Then Clay's voice dropped an octave. "Gail doesn't fit the profile of a capable secretary."

Just then, Liz knocked and showed Gail into the office. Gail's disorganized clothing consisted of a gray wrinkled full skirt, or maybe that was a dress under the long parrot-embroidered vest. Masses of hair not just past her shoulders but piled in heaps on her shoulders, stuck straight out from her scalp as if she hadn't touched the curls for five to ten years. Streaks of gray framed her forehead. She wore no makeup to speak of, except too much eyeliner giving her eyes a bruised look under her thick, rose-tinted glasses.

"My eyesight is going," Gail offered, fingering the ear pieces on her glasses. "That's why I quit the academy," Gail offered to Liz.

"How fast do you type?" I asked as Liz closed the door.

"I don't." Gail twirled a lock of hair between her fingers. "Men like me and I'm a whiz on the computer."

I smelled a sickeningly sweet perfume or mildew coming from the older woman's direction. "Do you know what to look for, for the police?"

"No," Gail smiled cheerfully. "I'll copy everything I can get my hands on."

"I guess that will have to do." I thought it was hopeless. Halloway wouldn't even accept this troll as a temporary, but the three of us trudged up the flight of marble stairs to his office anyway.

Outside Halloway's office, Clay stopped. "I smell rancid butter."

"Popcorn in a microwave somewhere probably drifted up the stairs," Gail said.

When I opened the double doors after a slight

knock, the odor became overwhelming.

"Henry Halloway, this is Gail Maynard," I said in a short burst of air.

"Creepy name," Gail said, taking the hem of Halloway's jacket sleeve instead of his hand as she took a step closer to him. "I'll be glad to be of service to you. Where's the computer?"

"First door on the left," Halloway said, actually returning Gail's smile. It was an unusual response. I half-expected him to balk at keeping Gail in his office. We stayed a little longer to see if he suspected anything.

"Captain Tanner sent me over to investigate about Chris Manning." Clay let that sink in, before going further.

"Been gone for a week." Halloway sighed, then rubbed his fat hands together. "My sources say the police have a missing person report."

I sat in one of the visitor chairs as if shocked. "I thought she'd be back in a week." I started to stand, wanting to make quick work of the meeting, but Clay shook his head no. "I hope Gail satisfies you," I added as I settled in for the long haul. A perfumed handkerchief was pulled from my belt for just such an emergency, pretending to wipe a tear as I regained a breath of air through the cloth's fragrant filter.

"She'll be fine." Halloway actually smiled again.

"The families of Pamela O'Brian and Claire Nemish asked for the autopsy reports." Clay spread his legs to secure more turf. He looked like he wanted to punch Halloway in his mammoth gut for no good reason other than the smell.

Halloway sensed the hostility and sought refuge

behind his desk. "I'd heard the bodies were buried on the mainland."

Clay and I exchanged glances. "You inquired about the disposition of the bodies?" Clay shuffled through his index cards, watching Halloway's reactions. "These three young women worked for you? Two dead, one missing?" Clay looked around the floor of the room as if he expected to find blood spots.

Halloway shook his head. "Anything I can do to help, just you let me know."

Unctuous bastard, I thought.

"Need to look through the girls' offices," Clay stated.

"They shared one desk." Halloway scrutinized his cuticles.

Clay took a chair next to me. "Their record books, appointment calendars, files."

Halloway choked on that one. "Do you have a subpoena?"

"Do I need one?"

"Oh, yeah." Halloway walked us to the door. "I'll notify the company lawyers. They'll want to be present, too."

Clay inspected a fake spot on the wall before exiting. "Be back shortly."

I noticed Halloway picked up the phone before we shut the door.

Halloway's oily behavior shocked me. "He knows something is up."

"Does he have a shredder?" Clay asked.

"Sure."

We headed back to my office.

But Clay stopped at the main entrance. "I've

already instructed Gail to copy every piece of paper before she shreds it."

"What if she's caught? How will she explain the copies?"

"She won't be." I thought I heard him muffle a laugh. "Did you like her get-up?"

"It was intentional?"

"No sense looking like you know what you're doing." Clay sighed. "Halloway prickled the hairs on the back of my neck. His eyebrows and eyes slant down." Clay ran his fingers through his unruly black curls. "I hope he doesn't use butter to slick down his hair."

Clay stepped around the workmen drilling holes into the virgin marble. He scanned the circular drive. "Are you expecting someone?" I struggled not to show my disappointment.

"A police car with the sirens at full tilt," Clay grinned. "I asked Bear to give me a lift to the station. Thought Halloway might breathe less easily if he thought I was part of the police force."

"Impersonating…?"

"That's where discretion takes a front seat." I heard the laughter rumble in his chest, but he squelched any outburst.

We heard the sirens coming. I knew Halloway would move to the window, blameworthy or not.

"Halloway harassment. How can anyone let themselves get that fat?" Clay asked.

I lied, sort of, "I haven't told my father how I feel about you."

"You do? I mean, you haven't? God help us," Clay said. "See you at Captain Tanner's at five?"

****

I estimated that the evening meeting with Captain Tanner would last through Mississippi's approved meal time, so I called home at two, knowing Mississippi gathered flowers for the table in the early afternoon. I needed to leave a short message, hoping to hang up before she could labor her bulky body to the phone. "Be home about nine. Tell my father." I did not want to be required to explain.

A question did come to mind whether I should consult with Liz about finding less comfort in calling Kani Nigel, Daddy, with Clay looming in my future. She'd say I was bragging, maybe prematurely. Only too clearly I could hear Mississippi's comment, if I troubled her with the news, "My Bible doesn't say there's an end to honoring your father and your mother."

At the mention of my mother, a dish towel would wipe away her sudden burst of tears. I didn't remember Karen, my mother, enough to evoke immediate reactions of grief. A more general, waterlogged-abandonment malaise claimed me. When I witnessed a mother touching her teenage daughter's hair, or the television advertised soccer moms embracing triumphant daughters, that's when I needed a dish towel or two of Mississippi's. Much to my embarrassment. If and when Clay witnessed one of my unpredictable outbursts, would he comfort me, or discount my grief? Who knew?

Driving north through Lahaina to the civic center, I speculated on what Captain Tanner might reveal about Pam and Claire. Turning off the Mustang's engine, rain suddenly descended in sheets.

I noticed Clay's MG had the top up.

If I didn't brave the rain to go inside, his police buddies would think I was late, or worse, disinterested. Refusing to be stopped by a fresh torrent of rain, I slammed the heavy car door and then sprinted for the station's back entrance. The door opened directly into the detective office area. Desks with no cubicles surrounding them facilitated the flow of information.

Bear noticed me first. He handed me three sheets of paper towels from the coffee stand to dry my hair. Apparently, all was forgiven after making Gail cry by giving her a job. I thanked him for the paper towels while I scanned the walls for a mirror. "Rest room?" I asked, preferring not to see Clay until I surveyed the rain's damage.

Bear pointed.

After taking care of business, I noticed no mirror hung over the sink. I dug out my compact and decided my damp and rumbled curls would have to do for the moment. I peeked over Clay's shoulder as he sat at a borrowed desk laying out a decision tree for the investigation with a chronological chart of future hours and fees.

He looped his heavy arm around my waist drawing me to his shoulder. "Billing one of the richest families on Maui doesn't provide the high I anticipated." I drifted in his admiration. "But seeing you does," he added with his trademark smile. Suddenly aware of the public display we were making, I pulled away.

Captain Tanner called Bear into his office. "Bring that couple in here and shut the door." Bear motioned us in and closed the door, with himself on the outside of the office. "Bear!" Tanner raised his voice to an unholy yell.

"Yes, sir." Bear opened the door sheepishly.

"Bring me those arson reports." Tanner motioned for me to take the only other chair in the room. "We tied down the license plate of the truck that's been following you."

"Arsons?" Clay asked.

Chapter Five

My fingers raked through my short, damp curls. "Arson," I repeated Clay's exclamation.

"How many?" Clay asked as Tanner examined the pile of file folders Bear had brought into the suddenly cramped office.

I wished Bear would open the door; the air seemed used up, empty of any molecule of oxygen.

"Maui's seen a rash of fires in the last two years. The fire chief and I finally agreed to look into each one." Tanner pulled out three files marked with red tags, nearly spilling the rest into my lap.

I righted the stack of folders while still seated.

There wasn't room to push my chair back to stand up. I breathed slowly, concentrating on the whirl of the air-conditioned coolness.

"Why would an arson suspect be following me?" I asked.

My empty stomach was flip-flopping as if I was on a roller coaster ride instead of safely seated in the captain's office.

Clay put his hand on my shoulder. "Pam and Claire's car was destroyed by fire."

"After driving off the cliff," Tanner corrected.

"Maybe it was pushed by the pick-up," Bear contributed to the bad news.

"Pam and Claire didn't own that car," I said,

feeling like a parrot repeating information everyone in the room knew.

I noticed I also dropped the tonal quality of my voice as if to match the base pitch from the men. Or maybe just the lack of trouble-free air deepened my voice.

Clay looked at Bear. "Have you found any previous salvage reports? Maybe the car was already junked before the pickup pushed it over the cliff."

"Whoa now." Tanner held up both his hands. "We're getting way ahead of ourselves. That license plate was reported as a witness to three fires. We haven't confirmed arson in any of the three. The owner is not a suspect. No sense in frightening Miss Nigel anymore than she already is.

Clay didn't bother to look in my direction, but apparently, Tanner noticed I was struggling for air.

"Who is it?" Clay asked.

His voice didn't hide the threatening tone that he had only played with in front of Halloway.

"Commons kid," Bear said. "We went to school with the whole crew. Five boys. The mother's never bothered to marry. Funny thing, the kids all look alike."

I coughed, trying to breathe.

The three men finally deigned to notice.

Bear asked, "Miss Nigel, would you like a Coke? We have Diet?"

I nodded, and removed my hand from my throat.

Wimps would be sent home and I was determined to stay until I had some answers. Thankfully, Bear left the door open when he left to retrieve the liquid refreshment. I counted my exhaled breaths: one, two, three, four.

"I'll get Pete to haul them all in for questioning." Tanner rifled through his top desk drawer.

I almost asked for the cigarette I thought he was rummaging for. It felt like I was going to fly out of my chair. I wanted to hold on to someone, or hide; I didn't know which. Fear was a powerful force.

Instead of a fag, the captain produced two search warrants. He handed them to Bear, who gave me the soda before retrieving the paperwork.

"Get some surveillance tape," Tanner said, "and take Clay and Miss Nigel out to the apartments of the girls."

"I'd like to listen to the questioning of Commons," Clay said. "Which one is it?"

"Vegas Commons owns the truck, but Boston's more than likely involved." Bear pocketed the warrants. "He's the oldest and the meanest."

"I'll videotape the interview," Captain Tanner said, sitting down for the first time and meeting my troubled gaze.

"Why would they be involved in arsons?" I asked.

Tanner scratched his head. "Young men, frustrated sexually. Who knows? Some psychologists say nutcases link sex and fires."

"You should go home." Clay steadied me as we walked to Bear's squad car.

"I'm fine," I lied.

I jumped in the back, then tried the car's door to see if it automatically locked, like on television.

Bear sniggered.

He caught my eye in the rear-view mirror and apologized. "Everyone does that."

"I need to come along." I put my arm on Clay's

massive thigh as he got into the backseat with me. "Or I might start some fires of my own."

"Don't joke about fires," Bear said. "People get hurt."

"Have there been any deaths in these fires the captain's talking about?" I asked.

"None," Bear said. "Probably why it took us so long to get involved."

"Bear," Clay said, "could you report on Chris Manning's apartment? Svetlana's already been there."

"Does Captain Tanner know that?" The squad car swayed as Bear turned to register his disapproval.

"I returned some personal items from her desk," I said, defending my actions. "And the landlady gave us the key."

"Still got the key, don't you?" Bear said and held out his hand.

"I meant to put the key back in the mailbox." I fished in my purse for the offending key.

Bear didn't move his hand, driving one-handed toward Olowlau; until I dropped Chris' key in his big mitt.

Clay replaced my key-freed hand on his thigh.

"Steady," he said as he let the weight of his hand over mine warm my cold fingers. The chauffeured ride to Hana also allowed Clay to put his arm around my shoulder.

It would have been too easy to weep, to lose any respect the two men might have for my input in the case. And there was absolutely no reason to experience a shred of fear. But I caught myself breathing in shallow spurts as if I was running up a flight of stairs.

"Is anyone following?" Clay asked Bear.

"That would be pretty stupid," I said, but couldn't help turning around to look out the back window for headlights.

"Not that I can make out," Bear said. "When I unlock the apartment door, take your shoes off. I've got extra pairs of plastic booties in my kit."

"Gloves, too?" Clay asked.

"Yep. Miss Nigel," Bear politely asked. "Could you keep the log of whatever we bag?"

"I will," I said.

I knew they didn't want me trampling all over evidence, which is exactly what I intended to do. Open every door, empty the drawers, the cabinets, the closets; read every diary, every letter; my mouth watered with the possibilities.

I asked them, "What are the chances of finding anything helpful?"

"Slim," Clay and Bear said in unison.

The darkening sky let the stars glitter on the moving ocean. Once out of the patrol car, we could hear the surf pounding gently. I buttoned my suit coat and Clay stepped around me, to buffer the cool ocean breeze.

Lights were on in the back of the grocery store. I felt like a peeping Tom as we walked behind the store to the second-floor stairs.

Once inside Pam and Claire's apartment, I knew we would find answers. I put on the plastic gloves and closed the open shutters. "They left in a rush," I concluded. Women would not want passersby to gawk into their rooms.

"Bikes are here," Bear commented. He handed me a clipboard and pen.

I watched as he directed Clay's attention to dents and a loose chain.

"Is that yellow paint?" The finger of my plastic glove indicated the spot on the edge of one of the handlebars.

Bear scrapped at the yellow paint, filling a gauze-covered pad with the flecks. He dropped the covered tablet into an evidence bag and I made a careful note on the numbered log sheet.

Clay was busy bagging and labeling glasses from the kitchenette's sink. The counter-divider produced one empty water bottle.

Bear used black powder to dust for fingerprints on the bikes and the medicine cabinet door. He kneeled to lift prints off a small refrigerator tucked under the divider.

Twin beds stood against opposite walls of bookshelves. Sturdy pillows transformed the beds into passable couches. The books included three small red volumes of *War and Peace*. The back spines were broken and glue failed to keep the binding secure on the middle volume. One of the young women used a rubber band to secure the back. Six volumes of plays by Christopher Fry stood next to a collection of Montaigne's essays, Marcus Aurealius' stoic dictates, and one tome by Camus. Biographies were shelved alphabetically: Disraeli, Goethe, Anais Nin, Bertrand Russell. A half-shelf of poetry included Emily's and a thick book called *Chinese Translations*.

"I know why they could deal with Halloway," I said out loud. "The women had depth. These were their treasures."

A cough from the next room made me blush.

"I would like to ask their landlord downstairs a few questions," Clay said.

"Better not," Bear said. "Have to clear it with the boss."

Empty spaces in the dark bookshelves were filled with driftwood and shells. I imagined living here. But, comparing their living arrangements to my own, reinforced my reluctance to move out of my father's home.

"Do furnished apartment landlords provide linen service?" I asked.

"Nope," Bear said.

I kept the evidence log tucked under my arm as I imagined their last moments in the rooms.

"No purses," I heard Clay nearly whisper to Bear.

A bad sign? Could be good. Either a thief absconded with their valuables or they left intentionally, without their bikes. How did the pickup's yellow paint get on the handlebars? Had he been harassing them, trailing them the way he had followed me?

I rechecked the medicine cabinet for things men might miss. No birth control pills. The bedside table's drawer held no diaphragm.

"Suitcases?" I asked Clay.

"Two big ones," Bear answered. He was on his knees again, fishing under the couch nearest the door.

"Did you find journals or diaries?" I asked.

Even though I was dubbed an introvert, I kept neither. I did scrupulously file my appointment calendars, all the way back to third grade.

"None," Clay answered and then asked Bear to bring in the mail.

I was glad to see no bills were included. The utilities must be part of the rent.

The postmarks on the first-class advertisements told us what we already knew. They hadn't opened mail after the accident.

I flipped on the light in the narrow hall which led to the bathroom.

Pam and Claire used the corridor as a flat closet, hanging their clothes on numerous nails. A few hangers were left empty. One hadn't been straightened when the garment was pulled from it.

I corrected its alignment.

Under the bathroom sink, I found wicker baskets holding a scant supply of underthings.

A gecko greeted my search with a scampering protest.

A shelf between the sink and medicine cabinet held matching red-and-gold Chinese cloth-covered round boxes. One retained a silver bracelet, the other kept three tubes of lipstick. I frowned at my reflection in the fluorescent-lit mirror. I didn't remember if Claire or Pam wore lipstick.

Bear dumped out the clothes hamper.

A pink blouse lay on the thin gray carpet. I remembered commenting to Pam about her good taste.

I hurriedly brushed a tear away.

Clay was at my shoulder. "Tape up the door," he directed Bear. "We don't want the landlord to saunter in here and disturb the place."

"What about blood?" I asked, pulling back the shower stall's curtain.

"The forensic team will take over,"—Clay ushered me out—"if the paint chips are linked to the pickup, or we find out anything more."

Anything more frightening than dying. I knew that's what he meant.

I was suddenly very tired and leaned on Clay. My stomach cramped from hunger.

Clay's arm automatically curled around my shoulder.

"Better get back to the Captain," Bear said.

In the police car, I wondered if we could trace outgoing calls on the phone Chris and the girls used at work.

"How long are phone records kept?" I asked.

"No phone in the place," Bear repeated.

"Have Gail look into that for us," Clay said, understanding what I was thinking. "Bear, tell Tanner that Miss Nigel and I are taking the ME out for supper."

That sounded really good to me. Hunger often clouded my mind. Now, it made juggling all the pieces of the case more difficult.

Pam and Claire might have been harmed intentionally, but I couldn't fathom any reason for the hatefulness, especially from a fire-addicted, sexually-frustrated set of illegitimate brothers, no less.

I followed Clay across the parking lot to the morgue. "Should I leave my Mustang here?"

We walked into Miss Windgate's office as if we owned the place.

I no longer harbored qualms about my decision to hire Clay Markin. Obviously, his days with the Academy afforded him valuable contacts.

We arrived at the morgue just as Miss Windgate was leaving.

"Penelope, if we buy you dinner,"—Clay held the

door open for her—"will you let us pick your brain about the car accident last weekend?"

"He has a way with him,"—Miss Windgate almost smiled at me—"doesn't he?"

"Svetlana Nigel," I introduced myself. "I hired the girls for their job at Maui Power."

"I understand," she said. Then she added in Clay's general direction, "I get to pick the place."

****

Over pasta Siciliana with calamari at Longhi's restaurant, Miss Windgate summarized her findings.

"Not official. The bodies took up space. I did a little more work than required for the substance abuse scan."

Clay reached across the table and patted Miss Windgate's bony, ringless hand. "The best part about you, Penelope, besides knowing fine food, is your curiosity. What did you find?"

I admitted to a certain wistfulness while I watched Clay court the information right out of the other woman. I wanted to be the focus of his quiet, probing charm.

"The bodies were charred, but that preserves the organs," she said.

I could see the case caught her interest.

"What did you find?" Clay slipped a white index card onto the table, and retrieved his pen.

"They died somewhere else."

I watched Clay write down, 'unknown murder site.'

"How do you know?" I asked.

"They both showed lividity on the front part of their bodies. Bruises on the back of their heads with

73

fractures underneath,"—Penelope paused for a bite of food—"as well as bruises on the brains…in front."

Clay raised both hands, looking puzzled.

"…contra-coup injuries," Penelope said.

Clay readied his pen. "In layman's terms, please."

She continued to eat for several more seconds.

"They were both struck on the head, laid somewhere on their faces for probably half a day." Miss Windgate's appetite was unconnected to the gruesome subject. "Then stuffed in that car before it was pushed off the cliff."

"You haven't informed Tanner or the District Attorney?" I whispered.

"The bodies were already scheduled to be shipped." Miss Windgate folded her napkin.

"But, Penelope, two murders were committed." Clay's fingers drummed the table twice.

Miss Windgate leaned forward, almost matching my whisper, "If you have any other proof, a motive, anything, write to the families and I'll bring out my notes." She sat back and straightened her spine. "Don't make me lose my job over this. Now you can drive me back. I have work to do."

"I won't jeopardize your position," Clay reassured her.

Now he was responsible for retaining two jobs: mine and Penelope's. "I appreciate the information."

Miss Windgate relaxed when we drove her back to the Center. "Let me go in and get the addresses of the families. Will that help?"

As soon as we walked back to Tanner's office, Clay called each girl's family. Said he was from the Kapalua Airport Rental Car's insurance company, and apologized for the late hour. "We would like to review the police reports, with your permission."

Bear refilled our coffee cups without asking.

Each family asked about foul play.

"In multiple-death accidents, the authorities make preliminary autopsies." Clay answered their questions calmly. "May I have permission, in writing, to look at the records?"

After the parents agreed, Clay gave them the police fax number.

We ran across Prison Street to the Medical Center to show Miss Windgate the resulting letters.

"Fast work." She handed Clay copies of her notes.

Bear stood at the back door of the police station waiting for us to return.

"Miss Windgate says the girls were dead when they went over the cliff," I said.

Clay handed Tanner copies of the case notes, then took a filtered cigarette out of the captain's mouth, broke it in half, and threw it in the trash can next to Tanner's desk.

"You suspect someone?" Tanner bit the hangnail on his thumb. "I can see it in your eyes, Clay."

"Penelope's preliminary notes don't point to anyone." Clay didn't step back from Tanner. "I visited Halloway at Maui Power. He's ugly as sin. He knew the bodies were shipped to the mainland."

"Can't get a warrant for ugly." Tanner sat behind his desk.

Clay asked, "You guys too busy with stolen tourist cameras to put a tail on him?"

"Don't get smart, kid." Tanner finished gnawing his right thumb's fingernail. "Halloway?" Tanner got back up and opened the small office's glass door. "Hey, Bear, bring me those complaints from the real-estate agents. I remember the strange name. This guy hasn't been making friends in his search for a new home."

Bear, twice as wide as Clay, loomed in the doorway. "Where'd you file them, Boss?"

"Don't call me Boss. I'm Captain to you."

"Yes, Captain." The giant tucked his head.

"Look in the misdemeanor files you were matching to those arson jobs." Tanner inspected the fingers on his left hand.

I could see Tanner's mouth watering for the next bite.

"Maybe your doctor should prescribe one of those patches," I suggested.

Bear knocked gently on the glass door and handed in a stack of complaints.

After spending five minutes shuffling papers, Tanner summarized. "Guess we've got enough here for a tail. Seems this Halloway doesn't like being told no."

Tanner handed the papers back to Bear. "You're sure Boston Common is a name?"

"Yes, Captain," Bear nearly saluted. "All the kids were baptized with mainland city names. Dallas, Vegas, Phoenix...."

Tanner interrupted him and lit a cigarette.

Clay wrote down the names. "Thanks, Captain."

"Call me Tanner." Tanner blew smoke into Clay's face. "Better get this young lady home."

"Would you mind following me?" I asked Clay, keeping my voice steady with an unfamiliar effort.

Chapter Six

Tuesday, December 18th

My hair wouldn't behave. Instead of curls, spikes stuck out in all directions. I watched my hands shake as I wielded both a brush and hair dryer through the mess.

Clay Markin said he liked red hair after we had dined with the medical examiner. He said that I was rare, that my hair genes were in only ten percent of the world's population. His exact words were, "We Hawaiians call you 'shu' because of your lighter skin, blue eyes, and curly red hair."

"Mississippi Huggins, our cook, says my eyes and hair should be brown," I had responded. "Father and Mississippi call me Sunny. I hated hearing 'Svet' in grammar school."

Hair color was a great subject as far as I was concerned. My thoughts tried to stick to it, but the faces of Pam, Claire, and Chris imposed reminders of their grim business.

Getting repetitive, Clay told me again that his mother's name was Tennessee Huggins. The conversation dragged on, so I told him again about my mother's death. "Abandoned doesn't cover how lost I felt."

"I understand," he had said. "That's why I don't mention my father's unseemly end."

I hadn't meant to laugh, nerves I guessed. Clay scowled. "Nothing can be that unseemly." I tried to explain my laughter.

He had smiled slightly, but only changed the subject back to folklore. "Mississippi is wrong about your eyes and hair. Distinctive descendants of pele personify the fiery volcano goddess, red hair and passionate natures."

Nearly every word Clay uttered seemed to my skewed thinking, slanted toward sensual subjects. Clay made me feel the Hawaiian mythology stories were closer to reality than Mississippi's cautions. "Aren't you afraid of my bad temper?" For some reason, my toes tingled along with the inside of my right ear. But we did not kiss again. Instead, he asked if he could call me Sunny. I told him no because he wasn't family and my mood was less than blithesome.

This particular morning, I refused to rehash any more of my newly aroused sexual yearnings. I didn't want to be late for work. With a final shake of my head, I sprayed it with environment-destroying hair spray and rushed downstairs.

My father waited at the foot of the staircase. "What's this?" He handed me a bill sent to him from Clay Marking.

"I'm late." I jangled my car keys. Clay said he would bill me. I looked at the address. Clearly Mr. Kani Nigel was not me. "Could we talk tonight?" I held the bill out for father to take back, without unfolding it to look at the amount owed.

"No," he said. "I'll walk you to the car."

"But, Father, I thought you agreed no accident was involved when Pam and Claire's car went over the hill."

The morning fog was going to make the ride across the island difficult. I would be late.

"That's not the issue." Father opened the Mustang's door and continued to hold it open after I put on my seat belt. He was determined to prevail. "I want to meet someone who has the balls to charge me two-hundred dollars an hour."

I shut off the engine. "Wow," I said. I couldn't help wondering if Clay intended to charge for the time they'd spent ruminating about Maui folklore at dinner.

"Tonight will be fine," Father stated.

"Yes, sir." I certainly wouldn't mind seeing Clay again. "I'll arrange for you to meet. At his office?"

"See that you do," my father said. Not even, have a nice day.

I accelerated past a reasonable speed limit in the fog, but I wanted to make up for lost time. Today was going to be a bear. For the first time, I hated going to work. Now I knew how ninety-eight percent of the world felt about their occupations, driving fast to a dreaded destination.

A good investment, her father deemed the money he sent to Urbana for tuition and expenses. I was thankful, and proving myself meant showing the money was well-spent. I meant to use the intelligence God gave me in a useful endeavor. I never anticipated murderers would kill members of Maui Power's staff. I hoped I could pull it off—look Henry Halloway in his diseased eyes long enough to gather more evidence. Was Halloway linked to the stalker, to the arsons? Not very likely.

But Halloway took a personal dislike to me since I'd first arrived on the job. I refused to complain to

Father. I'd already heard the speech about no one being able to hurt feelings unless you let them. Either I would die at the hands of some sex-crazed arsonist or I could choose to get tough enough to master Halloway's prejudice against me or my family—at least until we placed him in the cross-hairs of the crime.

I startled when my office phone rang. Nearly spilling the coffee Liz had just delivered. "Thank God," I answered Clay's questioning hello.

"What's wrong?" The concern in his voice shook me back to reality.

"Nothing, nothing. I thought it might be Halloway complaining about his new secretary." I wondered if the call would show up on a future bill from Clay. "Halloway clearly realizes we suspect some complicity in the death of his secretaries."

Clay spaced his words out slowly. "Right." There was another pause on the line. "I miss you and thought I might drive down to see your face."

"You know how to sweet talk, don't you?"

"I mean it," his tone sounded indignant.

"I'm glad," I easily relented. "My father wants to meet you tonight. Could we come by your office?"

There was silence for a moment. "Sure, sure," Clay said. "How about a drink after supper at the Pioneer Inn bar?"

"Okay." I smiled at the phone. "Then I can report on Gail's performance here." I heard a grumble and a shuffling of papers on the other end of the phone.

"I would have enjoyed seeing your face for lunch," Clay said.

I loved the low timbre of his voice. My nerves remembered the exact resonances he caused. "I'll be honest and tell you everything when I see you tonight." I tried to prolong the conversation. "Has Gail reported anything to you?" I couldn't put aside my doubts about the woman's qualifications and possible alcohol addiction. "Halloway doesn't need an excuse to give me a hard time."

Clay's voice dropped an octave, "I can come down there." His words seemed to punctuate the air.

"No, no." I couldn't help but grin at his protective tone. "I'm okay, really."

"Okay," Clay said. I could tell he wasn't that sure of my evaluation of the situation. "Call me after you talk to Gail," he pleaded.

"I'll see you tonight." I felt a qualm about the meeting. "With my father, Kani?"

"No problem."

I hung up and patted the top of the phone. Then I remembered a one-act play with Greta Garbo on television where she plays a mistress telling her lover goodbye. He's about to marry a younger woman. She wraps the long telephone cord around her body, letting it embrace her anguish. I shook myself. Good heavens. They'd only kissed and there were real problems with my friendship with Clay Markin. But, obviously, Clay had done his homework.

Father could afford the bill. After he sold his defunct sugar cane business to the Rutledges, he married my mother, who was heir to a much larger fortune from the Rutledges. Gossips said the marriage was probably part of the deal.

Kani was a fourth-generation Hawaiian mix, but I got the red hair directly from him. They were also the same height. Not nearly big enough for either of our tempers.

****

Liz knocked before opening the door to my office. "Gail's out here with boxes of copies from Halloway's office."

"Is he in the building?"

"Not yet."

I joined Liz and Gail in the outer office. A red moving trolley held eight boxes of paperwork. "Liz, we've got to store these somewhere, quickly." Always a page ahead of the world, Liz opened the storage room door and Gail shoved the cart inside. I stood helplessly in the doorway of her office. "Gail, could I speak to you for a moment?"

"No," she said. "I've got to be at my desk before Halloway gets in."

Gail didn't wait for my approval. So I ushered Liz into my office. "Liz, ship those boxes to the police department."

"Petty cash isn't going to cover the cost."

She was right. They could not get a purchase order for the shipment to the police without Halloway finding out. "Here, use my credit card again."

"I'll wait for Halloway to leave this evening and ask for a priority pick-up." Liz was as calm as I needed to be. "Do you really think he had something to do with the accident?"

Halloway pushed his way into my office. "I wanted to thank you for finding Gail," he said.

Good manners were my last refuge. "You're quite welcome. Happy to be of service." Halloway looked around the room, almost smiled at Liz, and left abruptly. I sat on the couch and hugged one of the yellow pillows. "I need one of Dumbo's feathers." I grinned at Liz trying to make light of the taste of real fear.

"You've been hanging around that giant of a detective too long." Liz punched the pillow I was holding. "Are they trying to scare you to death?"

"I'm being followed by a yellow pick-up that's been seen at the site of three arsons," I almost whispered, expecting Halloway to barge in again.

Liz sat next to me. "Holy shit!"

"I hate that word," I said primly.

"I'd hate it if anything happened to you." Now Liz sounded scared.

"I've been trying to link Halloway to the accident. But I don't think the police suspect him at all."

"Does Clay Markin?"

"Yes, but I think the basis of his dislike is Halloway's smell." We both giggled conspiratorially.

Then Liz clued me in on the latest. "Gail said she told Halloway to use KY jelly in his hair. He admitted to using butter. I guess it goes rancid pretty quickly in the heat."

"Well," I said, "Gail is certainly worth every penny we'll pay her to snoop on Halloway."

After we shared a second cup of coffee and glazed donuts, my first taste of food since supper, I called Clay. "You found me a winner." I congratulated him. "Even Father will be proud of you."

"Gail's good," he said. "Tell me about it."

"She copied a mountain of paperwork without Halloway finding out. And, best of all, she stopped the odor that followed him around."

"Was it butter on his hair?"

"It was," I said. "I better get to work. See you at about seven."

"One minute," Clay said. "Tanner called. Bear found that the VIN on the accident's car belonged to a car already scrapped by Vegas Commons. He's under arrest. They're grilling him now about why his brother, Boston, is following you."

"They haven't arrested Boston?"

"Not yet," Clay said. "Wear pink. Redheads should wear pink."

****

One thing redheads should never do is wear pink. Clay wanted to test Svetlana's sense of self. Sure enough, she chose a lovely shade of pale green for a wrap-around silk sundress. Her generous curves, accentuated by the smallest midriff and waist, made concentrating on his objectives difficult.

Gail took Clay's arm when they strolled over to meet Svetlana's father in the Pioneer Inn's bar. "Always a delight to meet new friends of Clay's." Gail made herself at home at their table.

Svetlana's eyes got bigger by the second, but her manners did not falter. "Gail Maynard and Clay Markin," she said, "this is my father, Kani Nigel."

Gail pulled Mr. Nigel down into a chair next to her.

Clay scooted out Svetlana's chair. "Good cover, don't you think?"

Svetlana gave him a fake, warm smile. "Excellent."

Clay could see Kani Nigel had sized up the situation correctly. "How long have you known Markin?" Kani asked Gail.

"Ten years," Gail crowed, "isn't it, love?"

"At least," Clay said, doing his best not to strangle

Gail. "Beer okay?" he said as he passed around the pitcher.

"Excellent." Svetlana seemed to be clenching her teeth. Clay thought he might have gone too far. He hoped Svetlana would understand he was trying to cover up his fledgling relationship with her. He wanted Svetlana's father to respect their business association, free of personal complications. But it occurred to Clay that Svetlana might have planned to introduce Clay as a suitor to her father.

"My daughter's been telling me you have some interesting theories about September eleven, Clay." Svetlana's father disengaged his arm from Gail's trifling.

Clay's eyebrows arched somewhat, but he went along with the pick of subjects. "I think all the conspiracy theories of the Sixties convinced people the FBI and CIA were all-powerful in delving into the motives of our enemies."

"Just chumps like the rest of us?" Mr. Nigel tipped his head to one side.

"Bastards just picked up their paychecks and hung America out to dry." Gail finished her glass and poured another.

"Motives don't always point to concrete actions." Svetlana poured a second glass, too. She looked angry and wouldn't meet Clay's eyes. Now, he remembered Svetlana telling him her father had no clue how she felt about Clay. And here he was, pushing Gail in their faces, making it look like Svetlana imagined a bond between them.

Clay tried to catch Svetlana's attention. "Did you tell your father about the case?"

She ignored him.

"We allowed to smoke in here?" Mr. Nigel asked.

Clay pulled out two cigars. "The verandah upstairs is best."

"Go ahead," Gail said. "Miss Nigel and I will keep the beer warm."

****

I sized up Gail's outfit. Clay must have a thing for pink. Gail wore hot-pink-flowered pants and a matching tight T-shirt showing off expansive but drooping curves. I cleared my throat with a swig of beer. "Ten years is a long time."

"Hey, thirty women is even longer."

I could not help showing my shock at the news. "Clay has had thirty lovers?"

"Isn't that many,"—Gail pulled her long hair over one shoulder, letting a cloud of lilac perfume and that mildew smell descend—"if you think of three dates a year."

"Oh, dates." My relief probably showed.

"No, lovers," Gail stated matter-of-factly, "and I'm still here, hale and hearty."

"Amazing," I said.

"How does it feel to be number thirty-one?" Gail laughed in my face.

My pride outdistanced my confidence. "Not bad when you're first in line."

****

Clay followed Mr. Nigel up the side stairs to his detective office's porch. "Beautiful night," Clay commented, unwrapping his cigar. They listened to the tree frogs tune up with the evening.

"Funny how different we are," Mr. Nigel

answered. "How tall are you?"

"Six-five." Clay wanted to add that Hawaiian blood didn't have height restrictions, but he maintained his respectful attitude.

"Your mother is Tennessee Huggins?"

"She is." Clay turned to the ocean to release a curling line of smoke downwind.

"My wife was a friend of Tennessee's." Mr. Nigel blew his smoke directly at Clay, then apologized and waved it away. "Girls like those white silks, don't they?" He fingered Clay's lapels.

Clay stepped back, bringing out his pidgin English to, at least, sound friendly. "*An' den*?" A gecko lizard creaked twice. Clay couldn't remember if that meant yes or no, or what the question had been. His stomach felt strangely jittery. "I've never been married." Clay wanted to horsewhip himself. Where did the word 'marriage' come from?

"Good." Kani Nigel stomped out his cigar. "Glad you understand my daughter is that kind; *da kine*, a forever person. I know you come from an honorable mother, but you have to understand that I will have both your kneecaps shattered if you touch my daughter without the benefit of marriage."

The sound of tree frogs had risen to an irritating pitch. Clay gave up on being friendly. Kani Nigel had obviously heard about his father's fate in Chicago. This shrimp only returned black looks, *stink eye*. "I do understand." Clay found his cigar didn't taste as well as anticipated. He stomped it out as Kani had, and tried a new subject. "*How you figga* Halloway? Do you want details about the case?"

"I better have every detail at these rates. We can

handle that over dinner at my place, without the suit, tomorrow night. *Lesgo*." When Kani rapped him on his shoulder, Clay felt like jumping off the porch.

****

I was sitting alone, trying to get the bartender's attention to bring over another pitcher when Clay and my father approached.

"Where's Gail?" Clay asked.

"Gone to bed?" My speech was a bit too articulated.

"Drunk," my father said. "My daughter is plastered, and it's a first. See you tomorrow for dinner, Mr. Markin."

"Yes, sir," Clay answered. He swiveled in my direction. "Shall I help you to the car?"

"Not necessary." I landed a wet kiss on Clay's cheek, catching him by surprise by the look on his face.

****

Clay retired to the back room to find a sulking Gail curled up in a corner booth. "What happened?"

"She said she's number one, and that I've been recycled."

"Great," he said in a neutral tone, meaning it with all his heart but worrying about the future of his kneecaps.

****

Wednesday, December 19th

Clay intended to clear the decks before arriving at Svetlana Nigel's for dinner with her father. He expected others to be as unjudgmental as he was. Kani Nigel's traditional statements in his role as a protective father let Clay realize taking Gail along to their meeting at the bar had been a bad idea.

Even though Svetlana said she told her father how she felt about Clay, he wasn't ready at that moment to accept all the implications. First, he attempted to shelve the declaration of affection under additional ploys. Contrariwise, he considered the possibility that Svetlana's involvement with the case would lend a temporary element to any affection she felt for him.

But now he knew she really loved him, from the tips of her unruly red curls to the ends of her sweet toes. Svetlana Nigel loved him enough to know he would be safe to marry her, with all his faults, with all his loyalty, with all his dreams for a future family. Somehow, he determined, he'd make it right.

Right enough for Kani to find him an acceptable suitor.

He downshifted the gears of the MG as he pulled off route 360 at the cut-off to 31. Parking at the corner of Uakea and Waikoloa, he walked slowly down Gail's street.

Clay planned his arrival as close to five o'clock as possible, giving him just enough time to set matters to rest before the specified 7:00 dinner hour with Mr. Nigel.

Gail wouldn't have the opportunity to down enough drinks to misunderstand him if he arrived close to quitting time. She was a dedicated worker on any of the jobs they'd been on.

In his inside pocket was a one-way ticket back to Australia. His watch told him he was too early.

Actually, he corrected himself, he was way too late.

Now was the time to be straight with Gail. Clay felt like a criminal. How could a person inform another human being that she was no longer needed in his life?

A scary thought dawned: what if he used women the way Gail used alcohol.

Inadequacies surfaced despite his state of denial. The attentions of fawning women were probably as intoxicating to him as Gail's brandy highs. Perhaps he grabbed women the same way Gail lifted her bottles.

But Clay knew in his heart the search wasn't for pleasure. He needed a sustaining love. One he would never desert. Someone like Svetlana.

He was not his father.

The aromas of Maui's plentitude of flowering plants, the bright colors of the various blooms set against the shifting shades of green, the sound of the surf, and the feel of the cool breeze from the glorious ocean—all punctuated the guilt Clay experienced.

Gail had a right to be on the island as much as he did.

Clay hung his head on the final turn to her house. Who did he think he was, king of the jungle? That made him smile ruefully.

"Heads up, Kupua man," Gail thumped his chest with her fist. "Don't look so surprised, I take the garbage out once a day."

"Howzit." Clay's mind tried to sort out logical sentences to present his situation with Svetlana to her.

"Let's sit on the porch, kiddo." Gail took his arm. "I feel as sober as a preacher's daughter."

He couldn't speak, didn't know where to begin.

Thankfully, Gail brought up the subject. "Besides your help, even if there are other jobs on Maui, I doubt anyone would hire me."

Clay shook his head to dispute that.

"Svetlana Nigel is a good catch, old mate." Gail let her shaggy head of hair fall over her shoulder, momentarily hiding her face.

Clay could not think of a comment, except, "Don't cry."

"I'm glad you came before I started drinking. I wanted to say mahalo, thank you for all these years." Gail pulled her hair back from her face. "You make me feel I'm worth the effort."

Clay fought back his own tears.

She patted his hand. "I'm not making any more promises about not drinking; but I think I'll give it a go, once we crack Halloway. But I want to try being sober back home."

She did wipe away a few tears. "I don't want to be one of those dopey women that visit their sainted husbands in jail."

"What?" he said.

"I think I'm falling for the guy everyone thinks is a bastard."

"Why?" he asked.

"Probably low self-image." Gail squirmed in her chair, embarrassed now. "What do you think?"

Clay handed her the airline ticket. "Open departure, good for a year. You might not want to use it."

"Always knew what you were thinking, didn't I?"

"I'll miss you, Gail." It wasn't a lie. Why couldn't they all just get along together? A childish wish in reality; Clay knew that.

"Don't let that up-tight bitch get away with boring you in bed." Gail grinned wickedly, then she got very serious. "Clay, people can hit you over the head with your own bat. Don't let them bedevil you about your father."

Clay shook his head. "I think I love the girl, Gail."

"I know you do, mate." Gail kissed his cheek. "It'll warm my heart knowing you're happy while I'm at home simmering in my own stews. I'll wait for this case to close."

"You're a true lady." Clay held her hand.

She pulled it away and went into the house without looking back.

Clay felt as if the weight of a mountain lifted from his soul.

He no longer needed to save her, as if he'd ever possessed the ability. The world looked brighter than it did this morning as if freshly washed by an overwhelmingly beneficial tsunami.

He checked his watch, plenty of time to get to Svetlana's.

"Thank God," he said, then added, somewhat humbled, "Thank God for life!"

****

Clay stashed his car behind the Banana Bungalow and walked the eight blocks to the Nigel estate on Mill Street. He didn't want to be followed or seen by any of the Commons brothers or their henchmen. Looking back in the direction of where he parked his MG, he caught a glimpse of the green and white Ka'ahumanu Church spire. Wondered if that was where Kani would want Svetlana to be married.

Maybe it was a good sign that the colors were the same as the Pioneer Inn. His native brain took over for a moment, giving into premonitions of good fortune. The future looked bright. Would Svetlana ever let him call her Sunny? Clay wasn't sure she would agree to his plans after the case went to court.

Would she marry him even if he'd been born a rung lower in society's ranks?

He tightened the belt on his khaki slacks. That damn Kani could grind his teeth if he wanted, but white silk did work with the ladies.

Clay wasn't that sure how to conduct himself around Svetlana and her father. If his hands strayed toward Svetlana, Kani might growl another threat. The pipsqueak! Crazy to put up with Kani's belligerent nonsense. Even for a well-paying job.

Svetlana would have to convince her father she could take care of herself. Shocked for an instant, Clay realized he would be the same kind of father, chasing suitors away from his daughters.

The Nigel koa-wood mansion was larger than Clay expected. The Nigels' Hawaiian cook, Bear's mother, opened the door. Clay wondered how he should address a second cousin who was old enough to be an aunt.

Inside, a balcony ran along the second floor of the house with an access grand stairway opposite a mammoth fireplace. The central section of the rooms seemed two stories high, up to a beamed ceiling. Shuttered partitions cordoned off sections upstairs and down.

He smelled a delicious feast as Mississippi smiled from ear to ear and pushed him into the dining room.

"Time to eat all this food right now." Mississippi indicated a chair for him in the middle of a gigantic table laden with food and flowers: golden ilima and fragrant white ginger ran the length of the long table.

Clay had never been late in his life. He looked at his wristwatch.

Kani and Svetlana jumped the gun.

Time held a recurrent effect and purpose in Clay's life, especially today. They'd started without him.

Fifteen minutes before he was invited to show up. What the hell was that? Damn if he'd let them rile him.

"Mr. Nigel," Clay nodded in Kani's direction before he sat down.

Then to Svetlana, "You look radiant."

Svetlana's eyes and face glowed in the candlelight and her lean shoulders were enhanced by a lacy off-the-shoulder dress.

"We just sat down." Svetlana pointed to a decanter of wine at his place. "Help yourself to a taste of Father's wine."

Hard to compete with a father who made his own wine.

Clay sampled the wine. "Superb," he directed to Kani.

Kani nodded his thanks. "The case?" His mouth was stuffed with food.

"Have you met Henry Halloway?" Clay asked him.

"Not socially," Kani said between swallows, "but he's an ugly son-of-a-bitch. Svetlana thinks he's involved. Employers can't be arrested because their secretaries come to a grizzly end."

Clay continued, "The medical examiner confirms Pam and Claire were murdered by blows to the backs of their heads before they were moved to the car."

"Any link to Halloway," Kani asked.

Svetlana spoke up. "Crime could be compensation for his looks."

"Not admissible in court," Clay stated. "Tanner is sending the paperwork Gail copied of Halloway's

94

spreadsheets to an auditor."

****

I watched Clay refill his plate with the dishes closest to him: tuna and mahi-mahi, purple sweet potatoes, and corn.

After one particularly spicy dish, he commented loudly, "Great cook!"

"Mahalo, tanks!" Mississippi was heard to crow from somewhere beyond the kitchen door.

"So far, Tanner hasn't linked Boston Commons. He's the guy who's been following Svetlana around. Anyway, we haven't connected Boston to his brother's ownership of the salvaged car where the girls were found. Except for the family relationship."

Clay let Father chew on that. "Or the arsons."

"Arsons?" Father asked. "Those have been going on for over two years."

Mississippi came in and handed Clay replenished serving dishes. His plate was heaped with food.

Clay seemed to hate talking. Probably didn't leave enough time for eating. But he said, "The only crimes Tanner could tag on Halloway were disrupting the peace citations. He's collecting a file of complaints from real estate agents about Halloway's belligerence."

Clay stopped to chew a bite. "…when the sellers won't take his unreasonable underbids.

Knowing the man, I said, "I bet Halloway makes offers on homes that are not on the market."

"Leaves a lot of homes in jeopardy," my father mused unhappily, "if he's linked to the arsons. Don't see how that applies to the secretaries."

"The police picked up Boston for questioning." Clay placed more sweet potatoes on his plate. "But his numerous brothers gave him alibis for the times of the arsons, and the police released him."

"How many brothers does he have?" Father had stopped eating.

"Plenty," Clay said. "There's Vegas, Dallas, Phoenix…. Tanner is checking out their stories."

"Evil exists," I said. "How is Gail this evening? I expected you to bring her."

Now Clay could figure out my reason for the rude greeting. I insisted Mississippi let father begin the meal early.

"Gail is flying home to Australia as soon as we solve this case," Clay said, looking me straight in the eye.

I showed my disbelief. "To visit her ailing family?"

"She plans to relocate permanently." Clay redirected his attention to his food. "Says she knows we're in love. She doesn't want to visit Halloway in jail." Clay held my gaze. "She's that fond of him."

"You have got to be joking. He's terrible." Then I remembered Halloway's creepy smile at Gail. "He's setting her up."

Clay tried to continue stuffing the great food down his gullet.

My father poured himself another glass of wine from the crystal decanter at his place setting. "A mainland trip to question the families of the secretaries might be in order, Clay."

Clay looked up at Father and then at my end of the table.

"Yes," Father said. "Take Sunny with you. You have a vacation coming, don't you, Sunny?"

"Yes, but Clay may not want me along." I actually

lowered my eyes.

"The families of Pam and Claire will more likely answer questions from a friend of the girls, rather than from some meddling, paid stranger." My father knew how to make a point.

Clay smiled in response to my suddenly changed demeanor.

Happy.

What could Father be thinking?

Clay resembled a spectator at a tennis match, switching his attention from my father to me.

"Hop over to Hawaii tomorrow morning." Father's expression at the opposite end of the table seemed pleasant enough. "I'll call work for you with your vacation notice."

"Thanks, Father." I couldn't contain my smile.

Clay looked worried.

When I rose, Clay lingered.

I waited until he finally let go of his fork and returned his napkin to the table.

Father remained to relish two desserts.

Clay reluctantly followed me outside.

I flung my arms around his neck. "Alone. We'll be alone on the mainland."

Clay coughed and asked, "You've been to the mainland?"

"Urbana," I answered.

I placed my arm in his, as we stood on the steps outside. "Father threatened you.'

"No," he lied.

"He told me he did," I lied and grinned up at him. "He's glad I'm meeting your mother before we go. My mother and Tennessee were friends."

Clay turned to watch the moon over the bay.

I wondered if he knew the smell of jasmine came from my perfume as well as from the flowers on each side of the steps.

"I'll set the meeting up for tomorrow morning." Clay patted my hand. "No sense putting off your father's directions. We'll leave for the big island tomorrow.

"What time will you pick me up?"

"I think seven would be best." Clay appeared reluctant to leave me.

My face was turned toward the moon.

I noticed in my peripheral vision that he stepped slightly to the side not to shadow the soft luminance in my eyes.

Never negate good lighting.

"You're a heart-rending image of eternity," he said.

The mocking word 'poet' stayed in my throat.

I willed myself not to move.

His hand strayed to my waist; the other traced the top of my nude shoulder.

I tipped my head up and closed my eyes.

His warm, full lips touched mine.

My body acted as if this was our first kiss. A Pele descendant, I admitted; a volcano flowed in my veins.

Clay held me close to prolong the kiss.

Father coughed behind us. "Better get going if you're starting out early."

When Clay shook hands, I was surprised to see a satisfied grin on my father's face.

"Kupuas take power when they shake hands," Father said.

I reached up and gave Clay another peck. "See you

soon."

****

Once outside and the door closed, Clay spread his arms out wide.

Was the kupua Kani referred to himself or…? Clay sobered with the truth, lowering his arms.

Kani was protecting his daughter from the Commons brothers or Henry Halloway. Murderers on Maui might not follow them off the island.

Chapter Seven

Thursday, December 19th

I couldn't sleep. First, I packed for every contingency for the trips to New Mexico and New Jersey this close to Christmas. I even packed my emerald green satin short dress for dining out on Christmas Eve. My jewelry-traveling bag bulged with jade and gold trinkets. I lined up six pairs of shoes before the truth hit me.

This was not our honeymoon.

We were on a case together.

I sat at my vanity table surveying the heap of clothing on the bed.

If I wanted to impress Clay as a partner in an investigation, I could start by carrying my own bags.

I put away the perfume, and emptied the jewelry wraps, except for earrings. For shoes, I chose one pair of dressy black platforms and an extra pair of sensible walking shoes.

By the time I re-hung all the unnecessary clothes and repacked sensible alternatives, I should have been exhausted.

However, my reclined body was rigid with anticipation. Clay's kiss convinced me he found me desirable. The night was long enough for me to realize that missing Clay would never be pleasant.

True, he might not have picked the best spy secretary for Henry Halloway, but that did not matter in the least.

What was important was that he wanted me for his mate, and I planned to be just that…for the rest of our natural lives.

At seven a.m. I opened the front door. The stone walkway parallel to the steps held an occupant.

Clay Markin, deep in thought, paced back and forth. He was clueless that I had unlatched the door.

I was not shy about interrupting his thoughts; I just enjoyed watching his body stride back and forth on the path. He preserved a cat-like grace for a big man.

"Are you walking to the mainland?" My flippant remark hid my anticipation. Soon, I would have this man all to myself.

Clay turned, his smile telegraphed that my outfit pleased him. "You know how to dress, lady."

"Green always does it." I pulled one bag over the threshold and hefted another to my shoulder. "Mississippi isn't up yet."

That was not strictly the truth, but I wanted to be alone with my man as soon as possible. "Should we eat at the airport?"

"Mother will have something for us." Clay relieved me of the shoulder bag without asking.

I wanted to handle both bags, but the truth was I appreciated his help.

Like every other woman on earth. I racked my brain to find a way to prove that I was different from all the women he had met, or would meet in the future. How could I accomplish that? Other women had loved him, according to Gail. The murders were, for the moment, not half as enthralling as the mystery of convincing Clay of my unique ability to make him happy.

Clay's MG lacked enough trunk space, so we ended up throwing a couple of the bags onto the backseat.

Intent on solving my conundrum, I was quiet on the short ride to the home of Tennessee Huggins Markin.

When we arrived at a string of garages near the foot of a hill, not far from Kahului, Clay hit a garage-door opener.

"Ready for a climb?" he asked, giving me a hand out of the passenger seat.

I was ready, ready for anything.

The hike up to the hilltop house provided two rest-stop landings with spectacular views of the ocean.

I could make out an extended roofline near the top. "Does your mother live in a tree house?"

"The architect insisted the house be built on a moving turret, so my mother could have a view of the ocean from the front room, kitchen, or bedroom, depending on which room she was in."

"Must do damage to the plants around it."

Clay stopped a step below me. "Smart cookie, aren't you?"

I put a hand on his shoulder and kissed the top of his head. "But I need a smarter husband."

Clay ducked his head.

Unable to see his expression, I kissed his dark hair one more time before heading up the last flight of wooden steps. Wanting Clay closer than any sparring partner could be, I decided not to continue futile verbal contests.

Above, dressed in a long, white eyelet dress, a small woman, close to my height, leaned over the porch banister. Her black hair was gathered in some mysterious way over one shoulder. The mass of hair nearly reached her knees.

I remembered her from somewhere in time.

Maui was a small island. Surely, our paths had crossed.

"Svetlana Nigel, my mother," Clay said behind me, "Tennessee Huggins Markin."

Tennessee took both of my hands, moving her warm grasp up my fingers. "No ring?" Without shifting her gaze to her son, Tennessee continued, "Clay, I thought you would only bring a girl to meet me that you were serious about."

She released me but not before adding, "Never mind, dear, we'll get him hooked yet."

Clay grumbled, "I should have added…my outrageous mother."

My heart raced.

I had jumped a hurdle without even realizing it. I was the first woman Clay introduced to his mother.

I instantly liked Tennessee and her gay abandon. "My father, Kani, says hello."

Tennessee only nodded. "It is your blessed mother I miss."

A sob caught in my throat.

After so many years, I didn't think I could respond with such grief at a passing comment. "Thank you," I mumbled, trying not to blubber.

Clay put his hands on his hips. "My God, Mother. Two jabs to the stomach in less than a minute."

"Oh, never mind an old crow." Tennessee hugged me. "Come and have breakfast."

Instead of following my hostess, I gawked at the house. "It's a miniature of my home."

Tennessee turned back. "Your mother arranged the building of the house for me as a commission for finding her a house on Maui."

"You're a real estate agent?"

"Was. I'm retired." Tennessee led me into the kitchen-dining room. "There's no more land available. Resale prices seemed obscene."

Clay had not waited for them. His plate was filled with eggs, bacon, and biscuits. "Dig in. We don't have much time."

I chose a warm scone and thick Devon cream as a topping. "Delicious."

"So why did you change the locks?" Clay asked.

"Change the locks?" Tennessee poured coffee for us.

"Tried to pick up more of my books, after I left the academy." Clay stopped eating for a millisecond. "Couldn't get in."

"Ten years ago." Tennessee joined them at the table. "You were gone. A delicate problem arose."

"What kind of a problem?" My emotions felt raw.

Flipping from joy to grief and back again left my senses on edge, waiting for the next shoe to fall on my head.

"An unwanted guest." Tennessee closed the subject with subtle evasion. "Tell me about this case and why you have to flee the island?"

"Flee?" I looked at Clay.

I felt uneasy, trapped by this family's habit of

allusive answers, and unanswered questions.

"Your father wants me to keep you safe from the murderers," Clay said, and added, "of the girls who went over the cliff last month."

"Murder, was it?" Tennessee offered me another scone.

I couldn't eat now. "I didn't know that."

"You knew it was murder," Clay argued.

"…that Father thought I was in that much danger."

Clay checked his watch. He did it regularly, nearly every half-hour. "Stories of being followed by the brother of an arsonist, who owned the salvaged car the girls were found in, probably tipped the scale."

"Clay, let me drive my Neon to the airport with you," Tennessee said. "Your MG will be well-hidden in the garage."

"Good idea." Clay folded his napkin. "But I'll leave your Neon at the airport. Finish up, Svetlana. I'll switch the suitcases."

Tennessee and her son exchanged keys.

But his mother did not let go of Clay's hand. "Honey, I'm sorry if you thought I locked you out. I'll explain later. You know I love you."

Clay hugged her, then rushed down the steps.

Tennessee called after him, "Thanks for bringing my future daughter-in-law over."

"Can't help liking you," I said, as we followed Clay down the stairs.

"You remind me so much of your mother," Tennessee said.

I hugged the warm-hearted woman. "I feel you've always been in my family."

****

On the plane to the mainland from Hawaii, Clay mulled over his frustration with his mother. How could she blatantly encourage this girl? Svetlana Nigel was a beauty and displayed all the manners a mother-in-law could ask for, but what gave her the right?

He had already decided Svetlana was the woman he would eventually marry. But Clay wanted his mother to know she had nothing to do with his decision.

Clay's worry settled down to the basics. Most of his mother's friends were day laborers or maids in the house of the best families. Tennessee rose above the lackadaisical attitude of her friends and family. She had more to think about than her next meal; she worried about his meals and his education. Clay knew not staying in the police academy was a disappointment to his mother.

Too many rules were just too many rules.

He knew his fixation with time had nothing to do with being paid by the hour. The comments about Hawaiians and errant schedules made him determined, from grade school on, that no one would ever say he was late for anything.

They could say his language gave him away.

Sure, Kani Nigel and he shared a lot in common, only different bloodlines, and different schools; but Svetlana Nigel had lived around money all her life. She knew how to speak with authority. Even when she was relaxed around him, her words were never as casual as his.

He could predict arriving at the home of her friends, once they were married, and feeling like an outsider, stupid among educated swanks. No amount of education would help. No matter how many books he read, his words would undermine his best efforts to be acceptable.

As if the imp of the perverse raged in his heart, the wrong words or intonations snuck out. He'd ask to use the john when he should ask to find the washroom. Something would slip out loud and clear: I'm not as good as you.

Clay almost admitted to himself that he tested other people's loyalty by purposely showing his uneducated, crass side. Childish, he knew.

Would Svetlana correct his grammar after they were married? Was she a purist who would embarrass him, or would she laugh behind his back with her friends?

Clay gazed at Svetlana as she leaned her beautiful body over him to view the departing islands. "Do you want to switch seats?"

****

"No." I kissed Clay's cheek. "I like to get up and pretend I have to use the washroom whenever I get a chance."

Even in First Class, Clay nodded his understanding and hatred of confinement. "My mother…"

"Went further than you intended?"

"Yes." Clay could not help himself—he touched my hair. "The curls feel like feathers instead of hair. Feel mine."

I placed my hand in his thick hair, then slid my fingers up and down his dear face, etching the contours in my mind, before giving his coarse hair a hard tug. "I like it. I like you. Are you going to make love to me on the mainland?"

Clay's body went rigid. "Your father!"

"Is not going to harm you."

"That isn't the point."

"What is?"

"We're here to do a job, not get involved." Clay smiled to soften the rejection. "Besides, you're not that type of girl."

"You'd have to marry me." I grinned and ran my hand down his leg, fingers inching toward his inner thigh.

Clay took my hand. "Slow down. Let's get the job done and see what happens.

I turned away. He did hurt my feelings, but Clay slipped his arm around me and I snuggled into him.

"I know you like me, find me attractive," I purred.

"Marriage is not a fling."

Was Clay feeling righteous, saving me from the worst in him?

"I want to be sure you love me," he whispered.

"Oh," I said, thinking about his excuse. "You want to put this junket on the right keel."

I looked up at him, continuing to gaze warmly into his eyes.

His body responded to the likelihood that I was his final mate.

Chapter Eight

In Sante Fe, the rental car decision seemed of no importance to Svetlana, so Clay chose the LaBaron.

His instincts told him when they were married, she might demand a particular color, but now she was all smiles: glad to be with him, touching his shoulder or his hand at every opportunity.

At least Svetlana didn't hang on him, like some of the in-heat dames he'd been around.

However, on the drive to Taos, she picked his brain on subjects he didn't want to consider, much less discuss.

"Your mother mentioned changing the locks after you left the academy."

Thank God she was driving and didn't notice the wince of pain cross his face. "Doesn't matter," Clay said.

"Your confusion, at the time, was surely understandable." She continued to poke at the wound.

"I'll tell you about that when I can command your full attention."

"Okay."

She then focused on his old friend. "I'm worried about Gail. Especially if she believes she is in love with that monster."

"She never drinks on the job." Clay stated the hope with all the conviction he could muster. Of course, he didn't mention the incidents at the academy when Gail was too drunk from the night before to show up at all.

"You don't judge people harshly, do you?"

Clay relaxed. "I see the tops of a lot of heads and the limitless domain of the sky." He turned toward her and rested his palm on the back of her beautiful head. "But the presence of some can change the surroundings in less time than it takes to breathe."

Svetlana chatted on about herself and the pearls of wisdom her sorority sister, Liz Cameron, would lay on her.

Clay struggled to keep awake, now that he was out of the hot seat.

"Do you think when I mature," she asked, "I will become less judgmental?"

Clay didn't bother to answer.

"I hope Gail isn't a loose cannon that we need to worry about." She tapped the wheel with the heel of her hand.

Clay tried to put a stop to the character assassination. "Sometimes a discouraging word can destroy the slimmest hope of opportunity for a person."

"I confess I have a shopping addiction for shoes." Svetlana laughed that delightful way he loved. "Mississippi says I am a reincarnated caterpillar. Do you believe Gail's opinions? That criminals are reincarnated for past sins?"

"Gail often confuses the spiritual program of Alcoholics Anonymous for spiritualists' beliefs." Clay endeavored to rein the conversation away from his old friend. "I believe in everything. Course, some say I believe in nothing."

"But you do," she said. "I can tell."

"The Creator knows what She's doing, even when we don't," Clay said. "I also know: no one should turn their back on the ocean."

Maybe to keep herself from dozing, she continued to ask a million make-talk questions. One was, "What metaphor would you choose for yourself?"

"That's easy," Clay said. "Copacetic, the calm of an incoming tide. And you?"

"Black water without a drain."

This time, Clay smiled. "How is that?"

She grinned at him. "I talk a lot braver than I feel and bluff around the edges of my self-doubts."

"Oh," Clay said, feeling protective and loyal. "You put on a good game."

Svetlana appreciated the compliment and smiled .

****

A dark panic seized his throat when he walked up to the registration desk of the adobe-faced hotel in Taos.

Two rooms, they would need two, down the hall from each other, if at all possible. Clay was intent on saving the reputation of his future wife.

The clerk was a young man, younger than Clay.

"Two rooms." Clay noticed his voice dropped an octave.

Svetlana, smiling, said to the younger guy, "With a connecting door."

Her smile would have melted a milkshake. They don't melt because of the plastic filler, which stayed upright in Clay's sink for two days, if he remembered correctly.

The kid swam in Svetlana's attention. "Absolutely." His voice quavered up an adolescent scale.

Then Svetlana followed Clay right into his room.

"Svetlana, we've discussed this," he said, still holding her luggage.

"Relax." She opened the connecting door and waited for him to bring the bags in.

"Just so we understand each other."

"No problem." Svetlana kicked off her shoes and started unbuttoning her blouse. "I'm going to take a shower and seduce you at my next opportunity."

Clay's brows arched and immediately backed out of the door. "I'll call Pam's parents and ask when we should show up."

"Depending on when they can see us,"—Svetlana turned on the shower in her bathroom and then peeked around the door at him—"why don't we pretend we're tourists with our free time?"

He laughed in relief.

Clay couldn't remember the last time he'd heard his own laugh.

"Deal," he said.

He took her seriously when she said she wanted to seduce him, imagining logical arguments against it, because, because... It didn't matter.

"Have you been to New Mexico before?"

"No," she called out.

Clay could hear the shower running when he turned back to his luggage.

Somehow, his silk suits seemed out of place in the hot desert. He pulled out a white T-shirt and jeans from his luggage. He needed a shower after being cooped up in that plane for hours.

He couldn't remember how long ago he had an

honest laugh.

Not since he left the academy. Not since he left his mother's house. A long time, maybe as a child. Yes, with his mother in an afternoon romp on the beach. He missed her. Men were not supposed to miss their mothers. He wondered what sort of man he would have been if his father was alive and not a gambler. Would he have had more occasions to laugh if his mother had remarried?

Turning on the faucet, warm water splashed his face. He touched the sides of his mouth. Still smiling.

Maybe ten years, all the hard time he spent around Gail. Not her fault. Mostly the job of a divorce detective could get a fella down, way down.

Life was changing around Svetlana Nigel.

Clay caught a glimpse of his face as he stepped out of the shower. That's what happiness looked like, on his own face for the world to see.

When he dialed the O'Brians' number to speak to Pam's parents, he remembered to keep the cheery tone out of his voice. He smiled at the sheer joy he felt impelled to hide on the phone.

Would life be perfect with Svetlana as his wife? He could put aside, at least wait, for his physical needs. Deserving her full acceptance was worth any effort.

As he hung up the phone, Svetlana appeared at their shared doorway, curls pert and damp, in a halter-top and modest, fairly long green shorts with a giant hat to match.

"How could you pack such a large hat?"

In spite of his best intentions, Clay wanted to slip his arms around that tiny waist, nuzzle where all the sweetness reigned.

Svetlana plopped the floppy thing on her head and twirled around.

She owned the fine, upstanding figure of a grown-up woman.

****

"It rolls up." I went over to the desk where Clay sat and pulled him to his feet. "Did you notice everything is pink in this place?"

"We can't see the O'Brians until tomorrow morning."

"If we find a painting we like, I'll ship it back to Maui." I stopped before we left the motel's lobby. "Are you hungry?"

"Aren't you?" he asked.

"Could you shop for an hour first?" I tried to ignore the rumble in his stomach.

I was afraid the stores would be closed by the time we finished eating. Maybe I wasn't the right wife material, not giving a future husband's needs priority over my own.

We must have gone through a hundred art shops, at least ten. I didn't find one painting worthy of shipment. Pinks and tans seemed to be the only color scheme worthy of the desert.

Finally, Clay couldn't wait any longer and suggested a restaurant for a luncheon break.

He asked for a second huge bowl of chili while I picked at a fruit salad.

"I guess a big man needs to eat." I tried not to let my eyes grow with every bite he took.

"And skinny dames eat like rabbits."

He was kidding, but my sharp intake of breath made him lose his appetite.

"Sorry. That was rude." Clay took my hand and stroked my fingertips. "Forgive me?"

"Okay." My momentary pout turned into a sunny smile. "Let's hit the crystal and rock shops."

"My feet," he moaned, then grinned at me. "Do you think you will ever get accustomed to my kidding?"

"I'll make you a deal," I said. "If you find something you like, I'll ship it back to the Pioneer Inn."

Photographed and painted sceneries did not attract Clay's attention half as much as rocks. Clay said he was paying homage to mother earth by purchasing her fallen teeth. He chose amethyst and the frozen sea foam of turquoise. He conjured whole universes from a split geode and immortalized fallen fossil leaves.

"I should have told you I would only pay for a painting." I furrowed my brow in mock frustration. "Those rocks are heavy."

"I'll pay for the shipping," Clay said. "I've got to have them."

"You are a rock hound and an interesting man," I said, reaching up to trace my fingertip down his nose, then along his jaw.

In front of the sales clerk and all, Clay gathered me into his arms and kissed my face. When he let me go, I confessed to feeling a little shaky, as if my sandals touched a floor going soft beneath me.

"My ears keep me dizzy after airplane rides."

"Take my arm," Clay whispered.

"Thanks." I gave him the full wattage power of my blue eyes. "You are hard to resist."

We walked nearly speechless until the moonlight dimmed. Being together all day, momentarily free of any other obligations, was heaven.

I swear he smelled good: male and a little sweaty, but enticing.

I liked being part of a couple, feeling encompassed by his affection. Tourists smiled at us.

I knew I was grinning and noticed Clay's face nearly shone with a new happiness I confessed to not seeing there before. I think the man enjoyed just walking along with me. Content, same emotion I felt.

At the hotel, Clay closed our connecting door.

I sat on the bed for a minute, then noticed my forehead was damp. Morality was not as easy as its billing.

****

Clay locked the connecting door from his side, then unlocked it.

A dim memory of his mother's locked doors and Svetlana's danger in Maui let him off the hook.

If Svetlana needed to climb into bed with him, she could.

****

Friday, December 21

Early Friday morning, Pam O'Brian's parents met us at their front door.

"Do you have news?" Mrs. O'Brian asked.

"Mother, let them in," Mr. O'Brian said.

The walls of the front room were lined to the ceiling with dark bookshelves. Clay settled next to me on a brown leather couch. The O'Brian couple continued to stand.

We're acting like a married couple, I thought. "Did your daughter mention anything she might be concerned about?"

116

"Pam sent us a box of papers. She said someone would come for them, eventually."

Mr. O'Brian left the room just then.

Mrs. O'Brian sat down in a rocking chair near the television and began to rock. "Do you know who did it?"

"We have a few leads," Clay said. "Could we ask that your daughter be exhumed for a more detailed autopsy?"

Mrs. O'Brian stopped rocking.

"For a more thorough search of clues by the medical examiner," I explained.

Mr. O'Brian returned with a large box, which he placed on the coffee table. "Mildred, they might like something to drink while they look through these."

"Sorry, I'm not myself."

After she left the room, Mr. O'Brian said, "She's nearly going crazy with grief. Pamela called her every night. My daughter was frightened. A yellow pick-up truck kept following them."

"He's still out there," I said.

"We have the license plate number," Clay said. "The man's name is Boston Commons. He's been following Svetlana since she first asked me to investigate."

"Is that the man who killed her?"

"Sir, we're not that far along in the investigation," Clay said. "I mentioned to Mrs. O'Brian that we need your permission for a medical examiner from Taos to go over Pam's remains."

Mr. O'Brian nodded. "Will these copies of purchase orders help?"

"We hope so," Clay and I said in unison.

****

After meeting with the local medical examiner to schedule the authorized autopsy, I felt somehow subdued.

Clay tried cheering me up.

We ordered dinner at an outdoor cafe.

He said the central fountain reminded him of the sounds of Maui that he already missed.

"Looks like Pam O'Brian did suspect Halloway of something," Clay said.

I felt catatonic, in a daze. I couldn't help staring at him.

"Are you angry with me about the separate rooms?" he asked.

"Of course not." I just couldn't summon a decent appetite, so I placed my fork on my plate.

"What's wrong?" Clay grumbled. "I hate repeating myself."

"I can't believe Henry Halloway would murder or authorize the murder of his secretaries. Why didn't he just fire them?"

"God knows," Clay said. "We'll have the auditors compare the purchase orders against Halloway's bank records."

"How would that explain what he wanted,"—I leaned toward him whispering the last words—"enough to kill two, maybe three, human beings?"

****

"I haven't been involved in a murder case before," Clay said.

God, the girl was beautiful, leaning toward him in her flimsy, flowered halter.

"They say you can't get inside the head of a mass

murderer." Clay wanted to peel her clothes off her. Instead, he continued the old saw. "Unless you want to think the way he does."

Svetlana leaned back in her chair. Her concentration drifted to the sidewalk traffic of arty-looking people.

"In Maui,"—Clay felt the disconnect of her focus—"land is the only thing unavailable to the average person."

Svetlana's ears pricked up. "Could Tennessee find out from her contacts if Halloway has been trying to buy land? Maybe greed was Halloway's motive."

"We'll call her when we get back to the hotel," Clay said.

He was enjoying how he felt around her—special. Important. Worthwhile.

Svetlana stood up. "Do you ever stop eating?"

The girl could dampen his mood. Then she got pushy.

"Come on." She tugged at his arm. "Let's get back to the hotel and look through that cache of evidence. Pam may have paid for them with her life."

They worked on filing the purchase orders by vendor until past midnight.

Svetlana's head bent over the task. "Did you notice how many orders there are to the water purifying company? The name is a bit weird too, Salome."

"Not for any large amounts." Clay shuffled the paperwork like a deck of cards. "Not over five thousand dollars each."

He read through the descriptions of work orders: sand dredging, water filters, oil slick containers. "The waste water from the plant has been mucking up Sugar

Beach Bay."

"But there must be over one hundred of them."
Svetlana drew his attention to the largest pile of papers.

"That's half a million dollars." Clay sat cross-
legged on the floor next to Svetlana's knees. "Too bad
we don't have Halloway's bank records."

"Your mother did say most of the properties
around the island cost over a million dollars just for
resale?"

Svetlana stood and paced the room. "Let's call
your mother and Tanner."

After they alerted Tennessee, Svetlana seemed
more cheerful...even playful.

Clay swatted her hand away from his hair while he
pushed the numbers for Tanner's office on the hotel's
phone for the second time.

"Are you going to help or hinder me in this
investigation?"

"Meanie," Svetlana said, then tackled another stack
of purchase orders.

"Tanner," Clay said, "we found purchase orders
from Maui Power in Pam O'Brian's personal effects.
She told her parents that someone would come for
them."

"Yeah," Clay answered Tanner's surprise. "There
are incredible mentions of a suspicious Salome clean-
up company. Contract work. Over a million dollars
worth."

"I don't know," Clay answered then repeated the
conversation to Svetlana, "Tanner wants to know how
we can link the company to Halloway."

"Svetlana," Clay nodded at her, answering
Tanner's rain of guestions. "No, separate rooms."

Clay held up his hand to get her attention. "Pick up the extension. Wait a minute, Captain."

Svetlana went back to her room.

Clay heard her pick up the line. "Okay, go ahead. I wanted Svetlana to hear this too."

Tanner repeated the news. "We found drops of gasoline around the bikes left in Pam and Claire's apartment. No reason for gasoline to be there."

"Was the yellow paint on the handlebars traced to the truck yet?" Svetlana asked.

"Not conclusively; same paint, but nothing unusual enough to stand up in court." Tanner sounded exasperated. "But the gasoline indicates that the arsons and the death of secretaries might be linked."

The captain promised to call them if he found out who owned Salome before they moved hotels.

When he hung up, Clay called to Svetlana, "I'm going to order something to drink. What do you want?"

Svetlana didn't answer him, so Clay went into her room and put his hand under her chin to get her attention away from the murders. "Hey, beauty, what kind of alcohol do you drink?"

She smiled at him, and immediately he melted into some spineless chump.

"I like orange juice and champagne."

"That's a breakfast drink."

He went to the phone to get away from her mesmerizing ways. "A bottle of brandy and two sniffers," is what he ordered from room service from her room.

Clay figured that at such a late hour, the waiter would take more than a half-hour to show up. Time enough for a cuddle break. He slipped his arms under

Svetlana's knees and around her shoulder, lifting her onto the handy bed.

Svetlana didn't resist.

He untied her halter-top and laid his head in her sweet bosom.

She sighed and kissed his ears.

That was too much for him. Clay ran his hands up the legs of her shorts. He wanted to touch…

The damn doorbell rang.

"What were you doing?" Clay grumbled at the surprised waiter. "Waiting down the hall when I called?"

Svetlana quickly dressed and resumed her filing job.

"That was fun," she said.

He offered her a brandy, mumbling about overly efficient motel staff.

"I didn't want you to stop," she said. Her blue eyes twinkled with need.

"I'm glad we were saved by the bell," Clay said, meaning it. This child didn't realize she had his number, all of them.

Clay didn't want to remember all the ramifications of drinking brandy in a hotel room with the woman his mother wanted him to marry and the woman whose father threatened to break his kneecaps if he touched the hem of her shorts.

"Let's give it up for the day."

"Good idea." Svetlana lazily rumpled her hair. "I can't even see straight."

She stumbled off to her room, through their connecting door.

Clay thankfully shut the door and then slid naked

into his bed.

He hoped she didn't misunderstand. He'd been straight with her about not wanting sex until they married, but then he turned around and encouraged her.

Would she ever see him as a person worthy enough to marry?

Clay wished he could just go for a swim in the surf. That always calmed him down. Without the movement of the ocean available, Clay felt as if his feet were on a listing ship. At any moment, the underlying motion of fate could overtake him.

Chapter Nine

Two hours later, I woke Clay with my screams for help.

He rushed into my room.

I was sitting straight up in the bed with my own hands around my throat. I couldn't stop screaming.

"A nightmare," Clay repeated again and again as he gently removed my hands from my throat. "You're having a nightmare."

I clung to him. "Don't leave me."

"Let me at least bring you a bottle of water." He made a swift trip to the hotel's mini bar.

I drank half the bottle with one hand, holding onto his T-shirt with my other hand. The cool water put out the raspy fire in my throat.

Clay reached to turn on the bedside table lamp.

"No," I said, feeling too embarrassed by my childish terrors to be seen.

He tried to cover me, but I hung onto him.

"Please. I'll be good," I pleaded.

I meant I knew we were both in the same bed. "I don't want to sleep alone anymore."

Clay laid down beside me and I nestled into his strong arms.

"Just talk to me," I said, still holding onto his thumb. I feared the memory of whatever caused those non-stop screams might return.

"Whatever makes you happy," he said. "Did you want to talk about your dream?"

"No." I could feel the panic returning.

In order to resume some semblance of mature sanity, I confessed, "When I get angry," I said, "I withdraw into a shell. My soul assumes a fetal position."

He held me closer. "Angry in the dream?"

"My dad over-indulged me," I said, cuddling closer, hoping he would stop asking about the damn nightmare.

"I would give anything to make you proud of me," Clay said.

"I love you," I said, exhaling a deep sigh, admitting my feelings.

Proud? I was not proud of Clay. Not that I was not thankful he was in my life. I did not feel personal pride in the fact that he was next to me in bed, or helping solve the case. I was paying him wages for that.

But I listened. He wanted me to be proud of him, besides loving him.

"The emotion of pride does not register in my relationship with my father." I tried to explain that pride was not an element of love. Was it?

Clay's muscles holding onto me relaxed.

"Mother says my best quality is integrity and compassion for others."

"I wish I could remember any of my mother's words," I said sadly. "I think one of the reasons I can't leave a store without buying too much is that I'm trying to fill the hole my mother left by dying, abandoning me on earth."

"Can I tell you my worst nightmare?" Clay asked.

125

"You may," I said, remembering Marcus Aurelius' instructions for correcting grammar.

"I'm ten and I awake at a noise, not the sea." Clay quickly launched into his dream. "They say I was big for my age." He changed position, rolling on his back and letting go of poor me.

"Mother's bedroom door is locked,"—his voice regressed to a much younger tone—"but I can hear subtle noises, whispers, hushes."

My own nightmare left the room like dust in the wind.

My attention focused entirely on the giant lying next to me. I wished now that I had allowed Clay to turn on the bedside light in order to follow the contour of his muscles that I probably should not touch, at least until the recitation of his dream was concluded.

The dim light from his bedroom's open doorway softened the shadows of his face. His tone eased, and I wondered if he would fall asleep before he finished.

"Sometimes," he said, "I fall asleep inside the dream. And then, depending who visited that night, will be stepped over, slightly nudged, or picked up and moved to my mother's disheveled bed."

Clay was using me as a therapist? Maybe not. Perhaps he wanted me to understand his distrust of women. Because his mother enjoyed lovers while he was growing up? I needed my psychology notes to figure out the best response.

I came up with, "You locked away your heart because your mother's arms were shared with someone else?"

"I knew you would understand." Clay's smile lit the distant ocean in Maui.

And I struggled with my native instincts, wanting nothing more than to nestle my nose next to his dear neck and smell his essence. I wished I owned a wreath of red blossoms for an excuse to hang my arms around his neck. I resisted lifting his T-shirt, yearning to slide my tongue down the middle of his chest. My saliva glands reacted to the imagined salty taste of maleness.

I thought Clay was continuing his dreamscape. "Remember the surf warnings the night I came to dinner,"—he didn't wait for my response—"I dreamt the nightmare that night. When I woke, a salty fragrance filled my lungs."

Clay rolled over and touched the top of my head. "I could remember the smell of your jasmine perfume," he said, "so I called my mother."

"You told her your dreams about being in bed with her?" I asked.

This man might have some serious relationship problems that I would never be able to cure, or fill, or relieve. But I liked him, the big bloke.

"No." I was privileged to hear his glorious laughter again. "But I did repeat my mantra, 'women know how to attract men, not how to love them,' before I called her. Even that didn't help."

"Help what?"

"I don't really know." Clay scratched his big head. "I know I'm looking forward to getting caught this time. Could be the Christmas season coming up with no family to call my own. I don't know. The machine answered at my mother's house."

I kept my silence.

Clay sighed, as if suddenly nervous to reveal more. "I didn't leave a message. I wanted to tell her I met a girl, maybe 'the' girl. I would have sounded like a four-year-old bragging about a new toy."

Or begging for attention, I thought.

Nevertheless, the big truth hung there between us, mutual attraction.

To change the subject, Clay said, "Sometimes at night I dream I'm a Maui King."

"Cool," I whispered. "Kupua men are shape-shifters." I did lift his shirt, but I only placed my palms on his bare chest.

"Kupua men take wives of sufficient beauty."—Clay played with my chin line, drawing me closer for a kiss—"in magic canoes transformed out of hibiscus blossoms." His voice seduced me toward his moving lips. "Favorable breezes take them to a private grove."

"I know this one." I kissed his chin. "You forgot, the little Mu and Menehune people who prepare a sumptuous feast for the marriage celebration."

Clay gave me only a peck on my mouth, and held my shoulders. "To keep a happy wife, a Kupua male must be an expert in fishing and farming."

"Ku is the ancestral god of production," I said, wrestling free and moving to lie on top of him, hands in his hair. "Pua is the sorcery goddess of possession."

Clay reacted to our closeness and rolled me off his body.

"Not until we're married. Right?" His eyes riveted me. "There's no surf to cool me off."

I relented and spoke of Maui. "Our island home keeps us constantly surrounded. Lands beyond horizon within the range of spirit voyagers are transmuted into dwellings in the air. They become the shapes and movements of the clouds, ever-shifting imitations dwell elsewhere on the good earth."

Clay's thudding pulse point under my palm relaxed.

He continued our folk tale. "The flights of birds, the sheet lightning, the swaying wind in the treetops, the cliff lines and mountain slopes cast their long shadows over the land."

I added the missing notes. "The roars of thunder, the patter of hail, and the constant sound of the sea break into many changing voices."

We missed our island world even cradled in each other's arms.

Clay didn't sleep for the rest of the night.

I did.

****

Saturday, December 22

On the flight to Newark Saturday afternoon, Clay was grouchy.

"Get some sleep," I said sweetly.

I was ready to redeem myself in Clay's eyes. I acted like a baby the night before, and he proved to be the perfect gentleman. Impressing him with my childish and wanton needs would only drive him away.

I touched the sleeve of his sweater, wondering if it was too late. He seemed so cold, even determined not to give me sway.

Maybe the murders *were* occupying his mind, but I wanted to be first in his thoughts, above everything else.

"Two rooms," he muttered from his nap.

Two rooms? Of course, this was a first for Clay Markin. He never slept in adjoining rooms with a woman he was interested in. Two hurdles were jumped without effort, without planning.

First, his mother's graceful acceptance of me, and now this. He must be worried about keeping my reputation unstained. Wives need honor.

I bet mothers did too.

That was why Clay was so upset when Tennessee changed the locks. But she was widowed for years. Clay was how old when his father was shot in a bar? What was he thinking, virgin birth? Then I remembered Clay's mother was deserted. They only found out about the husband's death after Clay successfully investigated the situation as a grown-up.

Clay started to snore.

Relief touched my heart.

He was up all night. I bet that wanting me and not touching me beyond the sustained comforting embrace after my nightmare, caused this exhaustion. Poor guy.

Energized, I was tempted to wake him, plan the wedding, agree where we would live... after the murderer was caught.

I slumped.

I watched from the airplane window as snowy drifts of the Midwest turned into the gray industrial patches of Eastern cities. What would they find down there from Claire Nemish's folks?

Once in Newark, I chose a red Escort rental car. It was late. The lot was dark and I thought the car was black.

Clay did order two rooms in the airport hotel without a connecting door.

****

Sunday, December 23

The next morning, we waited in the car for half an

hour in front of the Nemish residence. The couple said they might be late returning from church.

"My face is cold," I said.

"The wind can burn your skin as fast as the sun." Clay touched my nose. "Do you have a bit of powder?"

I marveled at how gentle this giant of a man could be. I wanted to know when he would propose. Probably not until they solved the case.

The Nemishes finally showed up.

In the glow of my affection, Clay Markin appeared courtly as he addressed the grieving couple, introducing first himself and then me.

Their gas fireplace came alive. Even without a tree, the front room glowed with holiday cheer.

"Neither of you is dressed for this cold," Mrs. Nemish admonished.

"Comes from living in Maui." Mr. Nemish frowned at their light wraps.

"The fire feels good," Clay admitted, stretching out his hands. "I remembered the sweaters but forgot we needed gloves too."

Clay's dulcet tones soothed the parents' nervousness.

"Hot chocolate." The couple nodded at each other and left the room.

I had to admit the warm cups and steamy sweetness chased the chill away, until I asked them, "Did Claire send home any documents for you to keep safe for her?"

Mrs. Nemish got very quiet staring at the marshmallows in her cup, while her husband left the room.

"Is there a real-estate broker with a yellow truck in

Maui?" Mr. Nemish asked when he returned with two boxes weighing down his arms.

Clay relieved him of the load.

"No," I answered, "but we are following leads concerning the owner of that pick-up."

Clay opened the box. "Claire didn't send home purchase orders. These are rejected, real-estate offers from Henry Halloway."

I explained what I knew about the girls' involvement. "I hired Claire and Pam to work for Henry Halloway. He's Director of Purchasing at Maui Power."

Clay put his arm around my shoulders and Mr. Nemish did the same with Claire's mother.

"We knew they lived together as more than friends," Mr. Nemish said.

"They were a great team, working on historical restorations on the island." Clay took over the conversation to give me time to get a grip. "Very responsible women."

"They would never have driven a car on Maui," I added quietly.

"That was the first thing that came to my mind," Mrs. Nemish said. She seemed to cheer up, just being able to talk about her daughter.

I looked at Clay, pleading with my eyes for him to continue.

"There is evidence they may have already been dead for a day." Clay's voice broke as he watched the sad couple take in the news. "Before they were placed in that car."

"We don't know where they were killed," I said as calmly as I could. "That's why we need to have more evidence from the bodies."

After we left the house of mourning, I said. "No wonder Halloway killed the girls. They secured enough evidence to put him away forever in a cheap metal box."

"We have to figure out where and when he killed them to convict him," Clay reminded me.

I held his hand after I got into our rental car. My arms wrapped around his neck, inhaling his scent. I never wanted to release him.

Clay put both hands on my face, kissing me gently and thoroughly.

I could feel his heartbeat racing.

"You love me," I said.

Clay did not answer with words; he only embraced me more tightly.

"Back to work," I whispered into his ear.

Clay let me go. "The ME will find more clues about where the girls died. I hope they're as good as Penelope Windgate."

"How old is Penny?" I asked, surprised by the jealous streak coursing through me.

"As old as my mother," Clay said, and then added, "and she's deeply in love with me."

"Not unusual for you, is it?" I couldn't help the testy tone in the words.

"Love is always a miracle." He started the car. "Look at us."

I figured that was close enough. "Did you notice how many of us are lonely children? Halloway is an orphan. Pam, Claire, even you and I are the only children in our families."

"I like children, keiki," Clay said.

"Bless your heart," I said. "Me too."

Chapter Ten

Monday, December 24

Christmas Eve in Maui found Gail Maynard in the basement of the Maui Power's office mansion, busily shredding paper for Henry Halloway.

Halloway asked her to work, promising dinner at his place after she insisted the sooner they delved into his past-life regression, the better he would feel.

"You're driving me crazy with all that jazzy talk," Halloway had said.

Gail felt a little insane herself. Telling Clay she might be in love with Halloway seemed almost truthful at the time. At least Clay might find happiness with Svetlana Nigel. As for herself, she doubted the excitement experienced around Halloway was really affection. All her senses seemed heightened as if life itself was passing too quickly. Her fingertips itched to touch another human being, her face needing kissing—other parts screamed their needs, too.

Fear apparently could mask itself as an aphrodisiac.

"I bind myself to silence when I instigate these happenings," Gail had told Halloway.

In her heart, she knew any information about paying for a murder absolved her from that promise.

Gail made copies of everything she shredded the

preceding night, just in case Halloway stopped by earlier than expected. He'd already told her he was an orphan, so she didn't think much of a family would help him celebrate Christmas Eve.

Her own family of forty-five first cousins was far away in Australia. Of course, her family drew names or they'd all be paupers. Most of them were poor.

Gail claimed it was destiny, that her family salted the earth. Without replenishment of spirits, encompassed by bodies, the world would be a sterile place. Incautiously, she believed most crimes were the result of not enough children in families. How could two parents, and sometimes only one parent, provide the attention a child needed to feel wanted?

Gail certainly felt her place on the earth was guaranteed.

Halloway was a prime example of the meanness of spirit that an isolated child could develop. Being number one, never having to share toys, and never being able to empathize with the secrets life demands to be shared, created Halloway's resentments. Greedy, ugly souls never knew acceptance long enough to look outside of themselves. Fulfilling the needs of others did somehow fill the empty bucket Gail often tried to fill with alcohol.

Working for Clay, even Svetlana, made her forget about the illusions of grandeur that she expected when she first arrived on the splendiferous island of Maui. Gail reminded herself to make an inner atonement for judging Halloway.

Only God was allowed to judge.

Gail re-tied her neck scarf around her nose and mouth. Shredding was a dusty business, especially if you were efficient. A drink would hit the spot.

When she felt sane, almost twenty days since her last drink, Gail tried to discern why alcohol remained in her life. Her thoughts, her brief time in Maui, everything might be different if she didn't drink.

The spiritual program of Alcoholics Anonymous confused her. People rarely spoke of ESP and paranormal happenings at the tables. Gail thought they were just too shy to share their experiences. Even her sponsor, a much younger woman, did seem shocked when Gail detailed past-life regressions as a method of healing.

In the darkened walls of the basement, Gail felt she was in a conjuring dance, a special zone of motion, feeding just enough sheets of paper into the machine so it wouldn't jam. After a while, she could almost hear the container fill. Each dumping operation caused more silt to fly around, settle in her massive amount of hair, dust her glasses and trouble her throat and lungs.

Halloway entered as she was finishing the last pile of papers.

The documents were mostly accounting histories of a dredging company, with a malicious-sounding name: Salome.

"Working hard?"

Gail wondered if she heard a tinge of malice in Halloway's tone.

"How else am I going to inveigle supper out of you?" She smiled as she undid the scarf.

Halloway brushed the dirt out of her hair by batting at it roughly. "Looks like it snowed in here."

"The cleaning lady will have a fit."

"That's what they're paid to do," Halloway

growled vindictively. "Clean up."

Gail kept her mouth shut. If anyone needed to clean up, it was Halloway.

She was constantly repulsed by the continued use of butter in his hair. After a day in Maui's sun, the odiferous stuff he used to keep the thin remnants of his hair slicked across his scalp smelled rancid.

"Should we expose your soul before or after dinner?" Gail asked with a veneer of respect.

"After," he said. "My car's out front. We can still pick up Chinese on the way over to Hana."

"I'll follow you," Gail said. "I live in Hana too."

"Oh, leave your car here." He smiled with all his yellowing teeth. "I'll pick you up for work on Wednesday."

Gail was sure she could count his molars. Wouldn't it be nice if she could enhance this personality that had been degraded by so much loneliness…if he was innocent of murder. His dentist could whiten his teeth.

She smiled genuinely back at him, believing people could catch the cheerfulness of her spirit. "I'll be right down. Let me get my sweater."

However, Halloway didn't leave her side.

Gail had meant to write a note to Svetlana and Clay to tell them where she had gone and why her car would seem abandoned on Christmas Day. Oh well, she'd just have to take refuge in her protective hedge of governing spirits. She inwardly called upon their help.

As Gail climbed into Halloway's Lincoln, she wondered why he was so willing to exhibit his torment in the regression therapy. The entity within him was troubled. She could feel its frantic heat.

"I decided to give in to your endless yammering,"

Halloway said as if he could read her thoughts.

"Please forgive me if my endeavoring to show you a way to relieve any psychic pain caused your discomfort." Gail ducked her head as if embarrassed.

Halloway changed his tone, a pathetic attempt at apology. "Got the better of my curiosity. Hold on while I pick up my order. Peking duck."

"Love it," she said.

Maybe she should disregard her overriding intuition of Halloway's insouciance. He must care about something.

When he got back in the car from the stop for Chinese food, Gail asked, "Do you like this side of the island?"

"No." he snapped, too loudly. "I've made offers on houses in Wailuku, but my credit line isn't up to the realtor's standards."

"That's a shame. I do like Hana. It seems more friendly, to me, than the people over in Wailuku."

"You would," he said. "You have a dreamy enthusiasm for everything."

"Thank you."

"That wasn't a compliment." Halloway pulled onto a rough gravel drive off Hauoli Street.

"I live on Uakea up north a bit. Your street name sounds almost like your name."

Halloway glared at her as if she was deliberately goading him. He opened the door to a much smaller home than she thought he would own.

"This is cozy," she said, using her best dewy-eyed look.

"F…." His remark left no room for comment.

Inside, Halloway stepped behind a grimy breakfast

counter and handed her a fork. "Dig in."

Completely cowed, Gail stood where she was and ate her Peking duck.

The windows were darkened with old-fashioned green shades. No drapes were in evidence. The floor was sticky beneath her feet and the carpet in the minuscule living room on the far side of the divider smelled as if a horse had died right there the night before.

Regaining a cordial tone, Gail said, "Did you want to recline or sit down when we do the therapy?"

"Therapy?" Halloway used his nastiest tone.

"Regression." Gail's courage carried her over most obstacles. "Some people refer to the practice as therapy because it is so healing."

"Come in the bedroom."

Gail took a peek at the gloomy, disheveled room and retrieved a stool from the breakfast nook to take in with her. "Okay, close your eyes."

"Don't you want me to get undressed?"

"You might want to take your shoes off."

Halloway rolled onto the unmade bed, kicking his shoes off, which thudded against the opposite wall. "There."

Trying to maintain a friendly gaze, Gail continued. "Close your eyes. Good. Now think of a pleasant place. Maybe one of the homes you bid on in Wailuku."

"Svetlana Nigel's place."

"I didn't know the Nigels were leaving Maui."

"They're not. I just want the pretentious place."

"I see. Well, think of the setting. Go inside?"

"I wasn't allowed."

"Okay." Gail was determined to keep focused, to

maintain the calm indifference this work needed. "You are going back to your childhood."

Halloway's rigid body experienced an involuntary spasm.

"You will feel as if you are falling asleep. When you wake, your energy level will be the same as a fresh morning after a long, dream-filled sleep."

"You're going to explain me away." Halloway's words were beginning to slur with sleep.

"You're passing back into your mother's womb, back up into the firmament where time has no earthly bounds." Gail thought Halloway was going to snore. His mouth stayed open.

She continued her directions for the ideal projection of his inner spirit. "Find the white cloud that holds the last pathway when you took an earthly body."

"There," he said as if amazed at the sight.

"Tell me where you're going." All the hope Gail experienced nearly blinded her.

"Ad Romam," he said, smiling in his sleep. "*eam ardentem videre possum. Quem illi omnes oderunt. Me abire volunt; sed illi ipsi flammis fumisque evanescent.*"

"Who are you?" Gail asked.

She recognized some of the words from four years of Latin: *ardentem* meant burning; *oderunt* was hate; *flammis fumisque evanescent* could be translated into everyone going up in smoke.

"Nero," he said, still smiling.

Gail didn't feel comfortable about leaving him connected to that memory. Maybe there was a more helpful life further back. "Let's repeat the process. Return to the upper regions of the soul."

Halloway sighed.

"Look around for your destiny cloud with the pathways that go back further in time."

"There," he said. "It's over a desert."

"Who are you?" she asked.

"Herod," he said with arrogant pride. Then angrily, "I miss Salome. When is she returning to the palace?"

Gail recoiled; the directions were not bringing out positive personalities. "Return to the past and come forward slowly. Find a safe harbor, where you are cherished."

"There are only onerous places." Halloway's troubled spirit writhed on the bed.

Inclement spirits filled the room.

Gail's fears mounted: her heart pounded in her ears. She wanted to run, leave the evil thing before her, a prisoner of his own sins.

Instead, Gail fulfilled her part of the bargain. "Come back to Maui now."

Gail knew she often mistook the psychic world for the real world, but this man's soul could only collude with tough customers. "Be at peace with yourself and feel a calming energy about you."

Halloway reached over and took her hand. "Has my history corroborated that I have reason to be angry?"

"It certainly did," Gail said honestly.

"Who was I?"

Gail wasn't practiced in being a dissembler. "Herod and Nero."

"Gail,"—Halloway swore for two minutes—"you've linked me with one man who uses women for sport and another who was an arsonist."

"In ensuing discussions,"—Gail gulped—"I'm sure

141

we'll find spiritual development for you through the dislocation of old ties to these entities."

"Can you walk home from here?" Halloway asked. "I'm exhausted."

Gail didn't mind walking home, but it was unusual for subjects not to feel energized. Could Halloway be enough of a swindler to satisfy her with definitions of past lives that fit the cold and deadening parameters of his personality?

On her walk home, Gail comforted herself. Halloway had not accosted her. His comments were vicious, but he was not a marauding terrorist—just a disappointed homebuyer.

She called Bear Huggins and asked to stay the night in Lahaina. Hana held too many restless spirits for a good night's rest. And Christmas was just around the corner. Surely goodness and mercy would follow.

Chapter Eleven

My Christmas Eve with Clay started right enough. Christmas shopping in New York was our only item on the day's agenda before catching the evening flight to Maui.

Clay knocked gently on my door.

"Yes?" I called sleepily.

"Rise and shine. I have coffee for you, if you're decent."

"Oh." I couldn't help sounding excited. "Bring it in." Room service from the only man in my life. "I'll hide under the covers."

Clay entered. "Sleepyhead, didn't you want to shop until you dropped today?"

"I did, I do." I accepted the cup of coffee, revealing my lacy green nightgown.

"Pretty fixings," he said, winking. "Should I order you yogurt or fruit?"

"Yes." Then I remembered. "I dreamt about your mother last night, or a woman very much like her. Or I recalled that she was around when Mother was in bed. Could your mother have nursed mine?"

Clay shook his head. "Everyone says they were close, our mothers."

Clay stalled, straightening the covers, and opening the blinds. "I ate before I brought you coffee." Then he listed the fare. "Two omelets, big slices of ham, sweet rolls enough for an army, two glasses of milk, and orange juice. Last time we went shopping, my stomach thought my head was cut off."

"What?"

"I really was hungry, so this time I prepared myself by eating enough to fuel any trek until lunch." Clay lingered at the door. "I've decided I'll cook breakfast after we're married; otherwise, I might just wither away from lack of nutrition."

"I do eat," I said, defending my eating habit. "Order more sweet rolls, yogurt, milk, orange juice, and another large pot of coffee."

A bit later, I opened his unlocked hotel door, dressed in a tan cashmere sweater and slacks. I thought they telegraphed the size of my bank account nicely.

"Wow," Clay said. "Pretty fancy for breakfast."

"I like to give the clerks an idea of what I expect to buy."

"What if I told your father I loved you?"

I was all smiles. "I'd like that."

"What would he do?"

"Congratulate me on finally finding a man I admire."

Clay smiled.

"What would your mother say?" I asked.

"Hooray!"

I mused over my yogurt, watching him eat six of the sweet rolls but, thankfully, held my witless tongue. Instead, I asked, "Have you figured out who your mother's visitor was?"

"No," he said too emphatically.

"What's wrong?"

"Why do you need to know?"

"I don't. What's the problem?" I blushed from embarrassment. "My curiosity just got the best of me."

Clay hung his head. "No, I'm the one to apologize. You need to know why I'm such a jerk about locked doors."

I maintained my silence, patiently watching his face change from one chameleon expression to the next.

"Mother raised me alone. I mean, she lived as if she was a widow." Clay struggled with his words. "Very young. In her thirties. My age now." A heavy sigh escaped his lips. "She had sex with people she didn't marry."

"Perfectly understandable. She didn't find anyone she wanted to be around her son."

Clay's face went blank. "You don't disapprove of her?"

"No." I perched on his lap and spread my fingers over his ears. "Your mother is a loving and very alive person. Did you want a nun to raise you?"

"No." Clay kissed my mouth. "Mother could have waited until she found the right person."

I kissed him right back. "Tennessee wasn't cheating on anyone. She was a widow. Oh," I said, jumping out of his lap. "You silly thing! You wanted her all to yourself."

Clay couldn't help laughing.

I hit the nail on the head.

"Exactly," he said.

"Well, never mind," I crooned. "You have me now."

"Do I?" Clay asked, grinning.

"Absolutely. When should we set the date?"

"After the trial."

After the trial? Clay's body gave every sign of wanting me to climb all over him.

"So we're sort of engaged, aren't we?" I'm sure he saw a wicked glint in my eye.

"You remind me of Gail when you're thinking of being ornery."

"I could compare you to my lovers, too."

"What lovers?" Clay stifled a laugh.

Now he was in trouble.

My hands rested on my hips and I faced him down. "Like the cad, who promised to marry me; the cheap rogue who stole my jewelry at college; or my mother's uncle who tried to rape me."

"Svetlana, don't," Clay cried, too loudly. "I'm sorry. It will never happen again."

I was still in a fit of pique, storming around the room, tossing his belongings back and forth.

"This place is a mess." I glared at him. "I'm not going to pick up after you once we're married. I work!"

"You don't think I work hard enough?" Clay's temper seemed to be getting the best of him. He lowered his head, balled up his fists, and sat back down. "Try to stay reasonable. All the sexual tension between us is sawing our nerves raw."

"How are you going to feed all those babies you dream about?" I went over the line.

"Now you're getting down and dirty." Clay crossed his arms. I could tell he was deciding to stay above the fray, stay dignified in his silence.

"You don't want people to murder each other just so you can stay in business, do you?"

"Svetlana, cut it out." Clay stayed seated, but made a supplicating gesture with his hands. "You don't want to do this."

"Yes, I do." I was still marching around the room. At least I stopped throwing things into his suitcase.

"I don't want my children fed with money earned by catching the worst dregs of society. Why do people have to kill others just to get what they have? Like Halloway's arson gang. Those poor girls."

"It's Christmas Eve, Svetlana." Clay attempted to shame me into regaining some semblance of sanity.

I started to cry out of anger. "I know you think I don't have any experience. I'm sorry I'm not a virgin. Those were all lies. Everyone in school thought I was stuck up. I was struck speechless with shyness."

"Sit over here," he said, patting his knee.

I did. "And I own a terrible temper."

Clay rubbed my back as I sobbed on his shoulder.

"I think we should concentrate on love-making today." Clay kissed my swollen lips, my wet cheeks, and locked his fingers in my curls.

"Yes." I sighed, with a gulp of a sob. "But I need you for more than sex."

"I know," Clay said. "I feel like a phony denying you pleasure, just to get you to promise to marry me."

"I don't enjoy being civilized," I said. "We need to pack and store our luggage with the concierge. Presents"—I kissed the bridge of his nose—"People expect presents on Christmas.

"Civilized people have sex," Clay said, maintaining a hold on me.

"Great hobby," I said.

He laughed, loudly. "We need to start making babies, cherub, moving into the future of the universe."

I remained quiet. For a second or two, I entertained

147

no thought of shopping. I felt in harmony with a world becalmed. Nevertheless, I talked him into his sweater and jacket.

On the taxi ride to downtown New York, we were privy to the mess a White Christmas includes. The white stuff descended in steady soft sheets. Six inches of dirty, slippery slush covered the pavements. Cars that looked like cupcakes with white frosting were slipping right through stoplights, horns were blaring and cars were barely missing each other. The less lucky drivers kissed the fenders in front of them. The collisions were at slow speeds, and the ruckus reminded me of an Urbana carnival ride of bumper cars.

Once inside Macy's, I faced Clay's reluctance to shop. My credit card was having a lovely time. Soft leather gloves for Clay, a silk bathrobe for Mississippi, and another expensive telescope for my father were shipped to Maui.

I suggested Clay stand in the long lines in front of cash registers to speed the process. He grumbled but took up the task with a heavy frown knitting his brow.

"Smile," I said. "Pretend you're Santa and we'll refill that tummy of yours in a few minutes."

A little girl held closer to her mother's hand when he grumbled, "Ho, ho, ho," at them.

An antique counter presented the perfect present for Tennessee. A fairly large emerald set in a gold leaf-like pendant called out her name.

"How much was that?" Clay asked when I told him the jewelry was for his mother.

"Enough," I said.

Then, to calm any fears of reciprocation, I added, "An antique green stone seemed appropriate for my future Maui mother-in-law."

Surprised at the emotion I felt, I sat down on one of the railings surrounding a Christmas tree decoration. "I might yet be mothered."

"You might finally see what the rest of us try to hide from," Clay said.

"Time to eat," I said, dragging Clay toward the busy restaurant lounge. "Mississippi says when the children are ornery, give them a cookie for each hand."

"I can buy that," Clay said, breaking into the first smile I witnessed since we boarded the taxi.

The restaurant's dark paneling reflected flickering, electric candles. By the time we were seated, I grew tired of the cheap decorations. Plastic greenery simulated festive garlands, while giant, pink foil-wrapped presents hung on a silver tree, promising empty Christmas delights.

"This is worse than going to Disney World for Christmas." Clay picked up the menu.

Hoping for passable holiday fare, I did the same. "I've never been."

"Let's make a promise never to go." Clay continued to read every word on the menu.

"Or, at least, never mention that we went," I agreed.

"To your snooty friends." Clay looked up to find a frown on my face.

"Why snooty?" I asked.

"Sorry." Clay reached for my hand but I placed it on my lap.

"Why snooty?"

Clay shifted his chair back from the table. "I hate being interrogated."

I was tired, too tired to brew up another storm of emotions.

"If I were home," Clay said, "I'd turn my face to the ocean." He sighed and his stomach growled. No time for a feast now. He had to face the music from his negative comment.

"I'm waiting," I said in my most acrimonious tone.

"Sorry." He smiled, knowing its power in the past.

I tucked my head, then leveled my blue, confrontational eyes at him. "Are you apologizing for calling my friends snooty, or for thinking they would act ignobly?"

Clay opened his hand on the table, probably expecting me to take it. "See, that's what I mean. Nobody uses the word 'ignobly' unless they want to put someone else down."

"Are you accusing me…?"

He had done it, again. My feathers were definitely ruffled.

Then I calmed down, but couldn't keep the corners of my mouth from turning up.

"We're having our second fight." I sounded triumphant.

"I don't fight with women." Clay turned gloomy, hungry.

"Eat something." I handed him the menu and motioned for the waitress. "Better bring this man some bread and soup while he decides what else to devour."

"Eat," he growled, then laughed loud enough to startle the departing waitress. "Our language could be a barrier."

"Nonsense," I said. "How can the words 'I love you,' cause any contention?"

The waitress brought the soup and bread.

Clay concentrated on breaking bread into his soup.

At least he knew to sit up straight and move the spoon away from him in the bowl, but he refused to give up breaking bread into his soup. "Manners, too."

I knew he meant his manners might complicate things. But I assured him, "You have a good heart. That is the basis of good manners."

The waitress intervened. "Are you ready to order?"

I ordered turkey, no gravy, cranberries, and a baked potato.

Clay, on the other hand, ordered mashed potatoes and gravy, dressing, turkey, dark and white, macaroni and cheese, corn on the cob, cranberries, and…, "Save me a piece of pumpkin and mincemeat pie. Could I have another bowl of this soup too?"

"Certainly." The waitress smiled at his enthusiasm. "I'll bring it right over."

"I promise never to correct your grammar or your manners," I said as if that would solve any future problems.

"Am I allowed to swear?" he asked.

"Of course," I lied, "if you find it necessary."

"Do you?"

I demurred, stalled in Clay's opinion. "I sometimes say 'shit' if I drop something or bump an elbow."

Clay was not buying that. "So when a dump truck runs into the back of your Mustang, you say love making, instead of F…?"

I laughed, a sound Clay loved enough to put up with anything that could possibly come between us.

"Why are we on this subject?" he asked.

"Testing the waters of marriage?" I guessed.

"We're not married yet."

"I feel married to you."

"You do not," Clay said, but I could tell he was flattered.

"I do."

"That's for the ceremony." He smiled, content with reality.

"Could we make love tonight?" I asked after the waitress was out of range.

"Is the case solved?" Clay mocked me.

I didn't mind his teasing. This man was mine, all mine.

"Beloved," I answered.

Chapter Twelve

Christmas Day, Tuesday

The snow continued to fall. Sounds of the city were muffled or lessened because of the blankets of fluff. As the white, relentless descent went on and on, the glory of overwhelming nature with civilization's ramparts dimmed.

Our taxi ride back to the airport lasted twice as long as expected. We planned for plenty of time to arrive, thinking we would dine in the airport's hotel, with an hour's leeway for collecting our baggage from the hotel in Newark before checking in at the airport.

However, when we arrived at the hotel, a somewhat worried or subdued Clay suggested we check the flight listing in the lobby.

Ours, along with the rest of the outgoing flights, were canceled.

The hotel's desk clerk informed us the airport was shut down until the runways could be cleared. Nearly all the rooms in the hotel were booked, but because we were prior guests, they would let us reserve the honeymoon suite on the top floor.

The price was exorbitant, but I accepted the charge.

We secured our bags and fought for a space on the elevator. Emptied of all the prior passengers, the top floor elevator doors opened to deposit us into a lush foyer of green-and-white striped wallpaper, white wainscoting, and thick flowered carpeting.

On a central marble table, the white flower arrangement matched the gold-framed floral paintings on the sidewalls of the room. Straight ahead, we could see the horizon of flickering city lights through a wall of circular windows above the king-sized bed. To our right, a small table was set for dinner with champagne already encased in an ice bucket.

The phone rang on the writing table to the left of the entrance.

Clay answered it and after a pause and asked me, "Would you enjoy duck with orange sauce, prime rib, or blackened salmon for our evening's meal? Apparently, the price is included in the room charge."

"I suppose the duck will do," I decided.

In addition, Clay ordered a prime rib for himself.

"So, when are we going to have sex?" I asked.

Clay didn't replace the phone. He looked at me and then at the phone as if wondering how the thing had ended up in his hand.

"No one will know." I reached for his hand, hung up the phone, and kissed him. "We belong to each other."

"I want to concentrate on you, have no other thought in my head," Clay said. "This case isn't solved."

"It is. We have the motive and the suspect."

"We don't know where Halloway did the deed or who he ordered to kill them." Clay moved his hands away from me when the doorbell rang with room service.

After Clay finally stopped moving his knife and

fork, he said, "I want you down to the bone."

Mercy, the man could talk. I smiled at him, convinced of his passion.

"We should," I said. "Did you notice we're starting to bicker again?"

Clay smiled. "I want to make lasting love to the only woman who could ever mean anything to me."

I began to unbutton his shirt.

Clay kicked off his shoes.

"Be gentle," he said, laughed, and gathered me up in his arms. He carried me over to the mammoth circular bed.

I pulled my sweater over my head, and Clay unzipped my slacks.

I felt like crooning some love song to him as he undressed himself standing next to the bed. I knelt on the coverlet and put my hands on his chest, my breasts cradling against him.

Clay wanted me, as if the dams of passion opened up on the equator. He tried to control himself to give me patient pleasuring before being swept up in the surf of emotions. His hands explored my secret places, sculptured my skin under his fingers.

My stomach churned as he delicately played with the most private parts of my anatomy. My curiosity was cut short by a surge of release. My neck jerked up, knocking my forehead into his cheekbone.

So that's what coming with a man was all about.

"Just getting started." Clay smiled down at me.

"I know," I lied.

His hands continued to gently manipulate my body.

I became aware of him pushing and rocking me back and forth. Inside, everything felt wet and welcoming. I gripped his hips and raised mine to match the rhythm.

When Clay came, I was riding on another wave of pleasure.

He cradled me in his arms, and kissed my wet mouth, now, always to be his.

"I love you," Clay said, as if the words ended a sob.

I nestled closer. "I will never tire of hearing you say so."

Clay kissed my throat, my breasts, my stomach. He ran his hands down my hips, slowly rubbing the back of my thighs.

My hands were in his hair; I was panting and shivering.

He put the palm of his hand on the lips of my sex, then spread them gently with his tongue.

The phone rang.

I clamped my legs against his ears. "Forget it," I said.

He couldn't. It rang on and on. Clay rolled away and answered.

Kani Nigel brought him to his senses. "Clay, your mother is okay."

Clay sat up. "My mother?"

I clung to his nude back.

Clay whispered to me, "Your father."

"She was shot in the fleshy part of her left arm," Kani said. "Trauma seems as bad as the...."

"Who did it?"

"Don't know but a yellow truck was seen in the neighborhood."

"Boston Commons," Clay said. "Tell Captain

Tanner to pick him up."

"I will," Kani said. "I told your mother you would be here by nightfall."

"Can I talk to her?"

"She's pretty upset, Clay." Kani's voice was gentle, consoling. "Do you want to wait until you see her?"

"Okay."

I could tell nothing was okay on the other end of the line. "May I speak to my father?"

Clay didn't relinquish the phone. "What time did it happen?"

Kani took a minute as if to consider. "Ten-thirty this morning. She called me after she called 911, but I got there before they did. I am sorry. Tennessee lost a lot of blood. They're giving her a transfusion. Clay, they told me she's going to be all right."

Clay forgot to thank Kani before ending the call.

"Halloway's henchman shot my mother," Clay said it to drive the reality home for himself more than to inform me.

"Two and a half hours before I ate,"—he gulped—"Mother was bleeding at home."

"Thank God she's alive." I needed to encourage him because guilt was written all over his face.

Clay could only glare at me. It was as if I had told him it was okay his mother was suffering.

"She called your father, right after she dialed 911."

"I didn't know they were that close," I said. "I am so sorry, Clay. If I had not gotten you involved in the case,"—my words ground glass into my stomach—"this would not have happened."

Clay looked confused. "Maybe she called Kani

because he would know where we were."

He didn't seem to blame me as much as I did.

****

Our flight left the airport at three o'clock in the morning.

I could understand Clay's anger, but not his coldness toward me. "Clay, do you love me?"

He turned his head toward the airplane window, away from me. "Yes. I do, but I'm not thinking much about it now."

I patted his knee. "Plenty of time," I said.

"Did you know frogs grow bigger in the tropics?" Clay's face was more relaxed, as if the non sequitur gave his anguish a break.

"Why is that?" I tried to understand any connection.

"The moisture in the air seeps through their skin and they thrive." His eyes were nearly blank as if he was talking in his sleep.

"Not like this dry airplane air?"

"I miss home," Clay said. His voice was deep with emotion. "What if I never see Mother alive again?"

I felt heartbroken for him, and for myself. What if we did not marry, what if something like this came between us.

"She will endure, Clay. My father is with her."

His head was nearly on his chest.

I could feel his agony without touching him.

"I've been avoiding her." Clay was talking almost to himself. "If that damn door hadn't been locked, I wouldn't have worried that she was angry with me. God forgive my pride in not calling her. I felt I had to prove I didn't need her...to be a complete man. I don't need her, but God,"—Clay took my hand—"how I would miss her!"

"I know." I hugged him. "Please, God, protect her."

Clay turned to me in his grief as a husband would a wife.

"You're doing the right thing," I said, "We'll be there soon."

"You liked her,"—Clay seemed calmer—"I could tell."

"My mother, Karen, and Tennessee must have been long-term friends. I wonder if she helped Mother when she was sick. I think I remember Tennessee's hair, of all things."

"Mother didn't mention a Mrs. Nigel." Clay straightened his suit coat.

"Wait," he said, his hand touching his chin. "Karen. Every second word was what Karen would have said, or what Karen thought about some issue."

"So they were friends."

An entire world of remembrances awaited on Maui.

Of course, my father and Mississippi talked about Mother; but Tennessee had been a close friend. I happily anticipated seeing her again. My future mother-in-law had been my mother's best friend.

"We'll be okay, Clay," I said, confident now.

Tennessee encouraged me to chase her only son. Deemed me worthy.

Tennessee knew the tree that bore me.

For the first time in a long while, I felt destiny favored me. Maybe Mother was looking after her only daughter, smoothing my way in life from the other side.

"I love you," I said out loud to Mother and Clay."

"I love you too." Clay bent down and kissed me sweetly.

****

The time spent on the plane from Newark to Denver and then to Hawaii's airport was torture for Clay. His efforts to pass time in conversation with Svetlana were forced, and even painful. He didn't want to show the most important woman in his life that it shook him to the core hearing his mother was injured.

He kept pinching his nose, surprised by the wetness near his eyes.

The air in the plane made his throat and tongue dry. Maui's air awaited him, moist and warm. No amount of cold drinks could relieve his thirst for his home island. New Jersey's winter didn't allow any bugs and Taos left creepy, clear scorpions among his discarded clothes in the bathroom.

Sure, Maui had mosquitoes, but the wise burning of sugar cane dusted their wings and slowed them down enough to smash. Besides, the constant ocean breeze kept the insects anchored to worthier objects than humans.

Maui held everything Clay would ever need.

Clay had come to a point in his life where his mother shouldn't mean as much to him as she did. The time-honored matriarchy of the islands still gripped his soul after all the years away from Tennessee's immediate control. A comfort it was to be a Maui man, heft the entire load without feeling abandoned by the other half of humanity. Women in Maui claimed their share of the responsibilities of life.

He turned toward Svetlana at his side. He kissed

her fingertips.

Svetlana smiled, alleviating some of his tension. "I'm glad it was my father who called."

"No one else knew where we were." But Kani didn't know the addresses of the girls unless he had contacted Captain Tanner before Clay told him to pick up Boston Commons. "By now the whole island knows we've been to the mainland together."

"Even Halloway?" Svetlana whispered.

"He'll know something is up as soon as Tanner picks up Boston."

"I have to go back to work on Thursday."

"Maybe we'll be able to arrest Halloway by then," Clay said, "if Gail has found out anything."

Svetlana nestled closer to him. "I have never felt as close to anyone as I feel toward you. And we've only known each other for twelve days. It's amazing."

Twelve days. Clay counted up the achievements. They'd agreed to marry… "Boss, your father may not agree with our plans."

"Boss?"

"I'm still charging you two hundred dollars an hour to find the killer."

"Even while you are sleeping, even when…?" Svetlana's body stiffened next to him.

"Eight-hour days," Clay corrected her, "plus expenses."

"How much do I owe you?"

"Over seventeen thousand and six hundred dollars, not counting expenses. I billed you for the first Saturday when we met."

"It's worth it to put Halloway away." Svetlana patted Clay's arm, letting out a long sigh. "If we can prove he killed Pam, Claire, and poor Chris."

"You could let Captain Tanner handle the rest of the case," Clay said, "then you and I can get on with our arrangements."

Svetlana gave him her million-dollar smile. "You don't like having a woman as your boss. Admit it."

Clay hung his head. Thoughts of his mother's constant directions as a young man in their home surfaced. "I don't vacuum."

"We'll hire a cleaning lady."

"Who cooks?" Clay's good humor returned.

He could do it. He could chalk off a hundred chores a day, just to be close to this woman.

"Not me," she said, her blue eyes sparkling.

Clay undid her seat belt, pulled her onto his lap, and kissed her into his heart. Mothers had nothing to compete with this feeling of oneness.

Svetlana pulled away and regained her seat, slapping at his hands as he tried to pull her back in a playful way. "Should we go to the hospital or your mother's house first?"

"Mother's," Clay said. "My car is there."

Chapter Thirteen

Wednesday, December 26

At Maui's Kahului airport, a wary cloud of apprehension descended on Clay as soon as we spotted Tennessee's white Neon.

"Please, Clay," I prompted, "if I drive, you can let the ocean view calm you."

Without a word, he stowed our suitcases in the trunk and buckled himself into the passenger side.

My hands were shaking, but holding onto the steering wheel masked the problem. Would Clay's mother still welcome me after what had happened? I knew Clay loved me, but his worry about his mother's condition complicated our relationship.

"If I wasn't so concerned about not letting my MG sit at the airport for a week," Clay sighed. "Mother would never have been injured."

"Clay, evil people can't rule our lives. If I hadn't been so vain to pack twice as many clothes as I needed, the suitcases would have fit in the MG."

"Dust in the wind," Clay said.

We spent the next five miles to Wailuku in silence.

Clay stared at the familiar ocean scenery, which normally soothed the most troubled of souls. He took a deep breath, and I shared the fresh ocean breeze.

Our silence let me imagine hearing the sounds of

the surf. But, I could taste the coppery flavor of Clay's anguish. The stupid case caused harm to his mother.

"Why didn't Tanner lock up Boston Commons when they found out his license number was the same as the truck that followed me?" I asked.

"Not enough evidence for even a stalking restraint," Clay said. "Besides, he could still follow me. Remember the law is the last refuge of civilization. Only animals shoot at unarmed women."

"So there are no deterrents, only punishments in the law." Fear crept around my knees, liquefying my legs to the point I was afraid if I walked, they'd tumble me to the ground.

"One of the reasons I quit the police academy." Clay directed his attention back to me. "There is really no conceivable way to protect the innocent."

I shook my head. "Well, I do not intend to live in fear." That notion horrified me.

"No," Clay said. His voice was sad, resigned. "Life is too precious for that."

When we arrived, Clay opened his mother's garage manually.

I retrieved the Christmas presents from our bags before Clay threw our suitcases on the back seat of his MG. I noticed dried splatters of what might be blood on the driver's side. My stomach flipped and my breath hitched, my body involuntarily shivering from the mental image of what had transpired. Clay came over to where I stood, apparently transfixed by the horror, as well. After figuring out what I was looking at, and without waiting for me, Clay raced up the steps to the tree house.

My father, Kani Nigel, stood in Tennessee's

kitchen. "Making coffee," he said to Clay, once we entered the house. "Your mother's lying down."

Clay didn't say a word.

I hugged my father hello, left the presents in the front room under an undecorated Christmas tree, and followed Clay into his mother's bedroom.

Tennessee was dressed in her signature white eyelet, sitting on the bed with plenty of pillows propped up around her. Although looking a bit frail, her strong character shone through.

"How bad is it?" Clay kneeled in front of her. "Will your arm be all right? What is Svetlana's father doing here?"

Tennessee laughed and motioned for me to come in.

I stood at the bedroom door. My face was flushed from intruding on a private moment between mother and son. His mother, however, kept motioning for me to enter.

"Did you run all the way up those steps after this bloke of a son of mine?" Tennessee patted the bed, inviting me to join her. "Let me say I'm okay."

She lifted and showed us her arm sling. "Doc said the wound heals faster if I don't move it."

"I'm so sorry." I stifled a sob. "I never imagined you were in any danger."

Clay stared at my father, who now stood in the doorway holding a cup of coffee.

Tennessee patted Clay's shoulder. "Get up, sweetheart. Let's go to the front room. We could all use coffee. Kani, bring the pot in there."

I questioned my father with a silent look, but he did not respond. Unusual, since he loved to crank his voice into all discussions.

Instead, he did Tennessee's bidding without a word, as if he had been at her beck and call all his life. Kani pushed a large disk on the wall of the living room. The house turned slowly, rewarding us with a view of the ocean.

"Crazy architect," Kani said.

"Mother loves the ocean as much as I do," Clay said, defending Tennessee.

His mother cut to the heart of the issue. "Kani is the reason I changed the locks, Clay."

Clay marched over to where Kani was arranging the sugar and cream containers on the table in front of the couch. My father ignored Clay's belligerent approach. "Cream and sugar?"

Clay nodded, un-mollified.

"I've been trying to court your mother since the year after Svetlana's mother passed."

Tennessee made a sweeping gesture as if that was old news. "I never had anything to do with him, Svetlana. Nevertheless, Clay, when you moved out, Kani decided it was time we got together. I disagreed and changed the locks."

"Mother's been dead for over fifteen years, Clay."

Actually, I thought my father and Tennessee would make a nice couple. Both were headstrong, carried themselves with confidence, and no one would push the other around.

"We fit together better than you two." Kani smirked up at Clay.

I saw Clay's muscles ripple, and noted the fist clench.

"Don't hit my father," I said.

Then we all laughed at the ridiculous scene, except for Clay.

Clay turned toward me, glaring, then seemed to resign his necessity to control the situation. He sat down on the couch with a thud. "Life keeps going faster than I'm ready for."

"I've been alone long enough." Tennessee patted Clay's knee. "So have you."

"Tell us how it happened," I said, changing the subject. "Is Boston in jail?"

Kani sat on the couch, closer to Tennessee than Clay. In fact, thigh to thigh.

"Yes," my father said. "He is. She called me as soon as it happened."

Tennessee looked at my father with deep affection, before saying, "I was bringing in decorations to trim the tree."

"He shot her while she was still in the garage." Kani leaned across Tennessee to speak directly to Clay. "The coward."

"Did you go to the station?" Clay asked.

"Tanner said we could wait for the arraignment."

"Did Boston implicate Halloway?" I hoped no one could tell how frightened I felt whenever I mentioned Halloway's name.

"Not yet," Kani said.

"We should get going." I stood in front of my father. "I need to unpack and get ready for work tomorrow."

"Clay can drive you home," he said.

"My car's a mess," Clay said.

"Take mine, dear," Tennessee said.

She placed her uninjured hand on Kani's knee. She

spoke as if to him alone, "When the resistance to love goes, so does a great deal of pain from the mental and emotional conflict."

She smiled at Clay and then at me.

"We have decided not to waste any more time," Kani explained further.

Clay stood up and put his arm around my shoulder. "I want to marry your daughter, sir."

"Does this mean you'll stop billing Sunny those ridiculous rates?"

"How much did he charge you?" Tennessee asked me.

"Two hundred dollars an hour," Clay answered.

I could see Clay was conflicted. To bill or not to bill.

Kani laughed.

I could not remember ever hearing my father laugh. Not ever. Did Tennessee have anything to do with his mood change?

"I plan to move in here with your mother, Clay. I will have my lawyer draw up a quick claim deed assigning my house to you and Sunny. Think of the house as a day-late Christmas present."

Clay plopped on the floor as if collapsed by the surprise.

I stood with my fingertips resting on his shoulder, feeling unstable myself. "That is an awfully nice wedding present, Father."

"It certainly is," Kani said. "Mississippi might agree to stay on as your cook if you don't give her a budget."

"She'll love working for family now." Tennessee included me in the Huggins female line.

Overjoyed with the turn of events, I clapped my hands. "We better trim this tree before Santa takes all our presents back."

Clay and Kani grumbled but helped more agreeably when Tennessee suggested that eggnog with or without a touch of brandy might make the chore go more smoothly.

Clay loved his gloves. He presented me with his Huggins grandmother's engagement ring, which fit like a blessing.

"Svetlana Markin," I said.

Kani showed his telescope to Tennessee first. "I haven't moved my telescopes over," he said to me, and then turned back to Tennessee. "They can wait."

"Tennessee," I asked, still holding onto her gift, "were you at Mother's bedside when I was young?"

"Yes, dear," she said, a sharp intake of breath inhaled before continuing. "You resemble Karen. Her hair was curly and strawberry blonde."

"I think I remember you. When I first met you again with Clay, I felt you had always been a part of my family." That image of her being with my mother blended into a memory that would remain forever in my heart. Cherished, the way Tennessee made me feel from the moment I officially met her.

I handed my present to my father. "Tennessee, this is from my father and me."

I hugged her and then took the present from Father's hands and gave it to my new mother-in-law.

"Oh," she said. "Oh. How did you know? Emerald's are my birthstone."

"Emeralds?" Clay laughed. "You told me they were green stones."

"And so they are," Kani said. "Shades of love and growth."

I was busy picking up used wrapping paper and adding the bows to the tree decorations when I realized this enormous happiness welling inside. What surprised me was how quickly other goals had taken a back seat to a primal urge. Solving the case seemed a secondary priority, and the constant rack of proving myself at my job in personnel seemed miniscule, even meaningless, compared to being alone with Clay.

Clay got back up. "Okay," he said. "As soon as we nail Halloway, we'll get married."

Kani and Tennessee exchanged glances.

Kani shook Clay's hand like men do, then slipped his hand up to Clay's elbow to show his affection. "I would feel Sunny was safer if you would stay with her, starting tonight."

"And every night until you're married," Tennessee hastened to add.

"That damn Halloway gang already injured one of my women." Kani appealed to Clay's protective emotions.

"Life is too short to stand on ceremony," Tennessee said.

Clay looked down at me. "If Svetlana agrees."

I rushed over and kissed Tennessee, and whispered in her ear, "He's all mine."

Tennessee hugged me and whispered in return, "This is for you."

The men could not see that she handed me a small pistol from the pocket of her dress.

I slipped the gun into my bag and powdered my nose for the men in the room, in case they wondered why I opened my purse.

Kani walked us to the door. "Clay," he said, "there is a New Year's Eve party planned for your new home. Why don't we call in the clergy and both get married?"

"If the case is solved?" Clay asked me.

"Or not," I said. "Our lives need to move on without a hitch from evil people."

A double wedding on New Year's Eve would give the tongues in Maui a real happy ending to chew on.

****

"Been looking for you two." Mississippi opened the door for Clay and Svetlana at the old Nigel residence, their new Markin home. "I'll put your bags in the master bedroom. Kani's taken all his things over to Tennessee's bungalow."

Clay couldn't move from the threshold. His house. They were going to live here. "I can hear our children running up and down the stairs." He pulled Svetlana to his side. "Should I carry you upstairs?"

Her beautiful laugh blessed the house.

"No," she said. "I know you. We'll go wait in the dining room for Mississippi to bring us something to eat."

Didn't sound that bad to Clay; he realized he was hungry for more than Svetlana.

The table was overflowing with flowers. Their place settings were at one end. The wine was chilling in a tableside bucket, and a tray of appetizers kept Clay's hands busy until Mississippi brought out a loaf of freshly baked bread and a tureen of fish chowder. A baked redfish, filet mignons, sweet potatoes, piles of peeled fruit, strawberry shortcake, and peach brandies rounded out the meal.

Clay resisted patting his stomach. He felt good. But mostly overwhelmed with happiness.

Svetlana hadn't rushed the meal, bless her heart.

"Enough," he said, grinning with satiated pleasure. "Upstairs."

"Showers," she said, racing ahead of him.

They stood face to face, hot water spraying down on their naked bodies, their hands exploring all the crevices of each other's body. Liquid soap made even the mat slippery.

"Stand still or you'll fall," Clay said, rinsing the last bubbles from her curls.

"As long as you catch me."

"Always," Clay said, sealing that thought with a deep kiss.

****

I wrapped myself in a long towel and headed for the bed.

Clay followed without the towel. He stretched out in the middle of the bed. "Your turn to dally."

I stood at the foot of the bed. "You're a very big man."

Clay sat up, embarrassed.

"No, no," I complained. "Be still. Did you know the soles of your feet are tan?"

"I hang them over the banister at the Inn when I don't have work." Clay wiggled his toes at my exploring fingertips.

"And this little piggy cried all the way home." I traced the inside of his legs with my fingers, then touched my tongue to the tip of his erection. Goosebumps immediately invaded his body.

An unexpected glow spread over Clay's skin as he

smiled down at me. "You love me," he said.

"What makes you think so?"

"Your hands give you away."

I had suppressed my fierce longing for Clay for what seemed like days but was more like twelve hours, creating quite a surge of hormones coursing through me.

In a swift movement, Clay pinned me to the bed.

My breath escaped in harsh gasps, hands raking and pulling at his hair.

Clay kissed first my mouth, and then the lips of my sex. He rested his head on my stomach.

I knew he felt the heat and the throbbing in my veins.

Clay lifted the slope of my hips to accommodate his bulk. Together, our thrusts maintained the same rhythm.

As if under a spell, I slid his hands up from my waist to my breasts, fighting for breath, matching his intensity.

Clay gasped when he withdrew.

Quivering, I pleaded. "Don't tease."

He drew me to him again, vibrating with the fire kindled in his loins. His hands slid under my arms, down my thighs, up amongst my curls.

"I can't wait," he said sadly, as he kissed my mouth and came deep inside.

My body jolted beneath Clay as the nerves released down my spine throughout my pelvis.

I teased him with a pout. "When do we get to repeat that?"

"When I'm no longer experiencing ecstasy." Clay reached for the phone, and uncradled the earpiece.

"Okay," I laughed, tantalizing him with a whispered promise.

We slept from the strain of scoured and snagged nerves. But also from our deep, satisfying sexual experience.

Once, maybe twice, I roused him during the night and our shared sensations heightened the pounding pace of our hearts.

Chapter Fourteen

Wednesday, December 26

Chris Manning returned to her efficiency to find yellow crime tape covering her door. She ripped it off, thinking the neighbor's teenaged sons were playing a joke.

Inside, she wasn't laughing when she found her belongings in disarray and fingerprint dusting powder all over everything. Her stacks of books surrounding the room were now tipped over in eddies left from the invasion.

A box filled with her office things sat on the bed. She read Liz and Svetlana's note.

Without sitting down, she called 911, only to be asked to come in for questioning for her own missing person's report. "You guys are so stupid. It's me. I'm the one calling you. Jeez."

She hung up and called work. Sure, it was the day after Christmas, but if the idiot police had lost her job for her, she was in big trouble.

The personnel office didn't answer, so she called her old desk.

"I knew you'd show up." Gail Maynard introduced herself.

"Who said anything was wrong?" Chris's initial anger at the people on the other end of 911 still raged within her.

"That prissy dame in personnel."

"Svetlana Nigel?" She liked Svetlana.

However, she hadn't spoken directly to Svetlana before leaving for Florida. Maybe she'd been worried.

"My mother died in Florida." Chris sat on the edge of her bed, trying not to sob to this stranger. "I had to leave immediately or I would have missed the funeral. I left a message."

"I'm sorry."

A long, heavy exhale later, Chris asked, "Did they hire you for my job?"

"Only temporarily," Gail said. "You might as well show up today and get everything straightened out."

"Okay." Chris glanced at herself in the mirror. If she added a jacket, no one would notice her blouse was somewhat wrinkled. "Guess I should call the police back."

"I guess you better." Chris heard Gail laugh. "They're trying to pin your murder on your boss."

"On ugly Halloway?"

"Hey, I like him." Gail sounded personally insulted.

"You do?" Chris couldn't help recalling the overwhelming odor of Halloway. "Are my candles still on the desk?"

"In those cute wooden houses?" the older-sounding woman asked. "I haven't used them."

That surprised Chris. She had to light each candle every day, just to stay at her desk outside Halloway's office. "Maybe I should let you keep the job."

"You will show up today?" Gail asked. "Promise?"

"Sure," Chris said.

It wasn't as if she had received an inheritance or anything.

But Chris didn't call the police again. They were rude the first time and didn't believe her claim who she was.

Besides, she was already late for work.

Chris's unplaced phone call would cost Gail Maynard.

****

Once the call ended, Gail realized how tired she was of being a mediator between the police and Henry Halloway. She wasn't that lazy, but showing up for work at eight a.m. every day was a drag.

Her previous indolent lifestyle as a guru for less intuitive women paid nothing. Clay's work and Bear Huggins' generosity kept her well fed. It took a lot of energy to keep Halloway deluded. Her natural lassitude balked at the constant beguiling that never seemed to alleviate Halloway's sneer, anyway.

Australia beckoned.

Gail planned to tell Bear Huggins about Clay's airline ticket. Not as brilliant as Clay, the six-foot-eight-inch giant was a gentleman. Bear skirted the sex issue by substituting all-night embraces. Gail giggled to think of being named Gail Huggins.

Henry Halloway was twice the man Bear could ever be. Bear reminded her of a child. He probably was a virgin. She felt safe around him, like one of her many brothers in Australia.

What she really wanted was a drink, but a promise to Clay was a promise.

At least she knew Halloway had nothing to do with his secretaries getting killed in a car accident. That was the trouble with these obsessive revolutionaries. They were stubborn. Ordinary people didn't expect folks like Pam and Claire to accomplish normal things, like getting in a car on a rainy day and then driving off the cliff.

Gail placed her hair into a knot and used the desk scissors to cut a chunk of it away. Better than yanking the roots out. She threw the chunk of hair in the wastebasket.

Chris Manning's reappearance should have alleviated all her fears, but a bell was ringing somewhere she wanted to ignore.

She decided to ask Liz Cameron out to lunch. Maybe Bear would come too. They might like each other.

She called Bear first. "Will you be able to see me for lunch today?"

Agreeing, he said he'd meet her at the Kihei terrace restaurant.

Gail headed down to ask Liz to join them. Liz was another stuck-up kid, but not as bad as that Svetlana chick.

****

Liz Cameron admitted she did not approve of Gail Maynard working for Henry Halloway. She knew Svetlana and Clay Markin were playing some sort of espionage game, but they should never have picked Gail to help them. Something about the woman seemed off-kilter. Both of Gail's oars were not in the water.

Of course, thinking is a powerful magnet, and Gail showed up as the first visitor of the day. Dressed in embroidered jeans with a peasant blouse, Gail plunked her completely inappropriate bottom down in the chair next to Liz's desk.

"Chris Manning called me upstairs," Gail said. "She's coming in today."

"Where was she?" Liz reached for the phone.

Gail shook her head to stop her. "Chris has already spoken to the police."

"Where did she go?" Liz tried to find refuge in politeness. She wanted to shake the frumpy woman to get the vital information.

"She was notified of her mother's death after working hours." Gail unsecured a loose pile of hair at the nape and then fluffed the entire mass, which emitted a cloud of dandruff.

Liz felt like dusting off the desk but restrained herself.

Gail continued, feigning not to notice the significant amount of scalp debris that littered Liz's desk. "Chris said she left a message that she'd gone to the funeral in Florida."

Liz remembered the message system had been down that one weekend.

"Would you join me for lunch?" Gail smiled and touched Liz's forearm. "Clay and Svetlana aren't scheduled to return to Maui until tomorrow, and I'm so excited about Halloway being innocent."

Liz hid her horror at the thought of eating anywhere near that unruly head of hair and kinky thought patterns. The woman appeared to be clean, but a mildew odor rafted uneasily around her. Not appetizing in the least.

"Sure," Liz said.

"I'll need to ride with you," Gail added as she left.

Lunch at the Kihei terrace promised to be noisy.

The fenced-in patio provided a haven for toddlers while their mothers caught up on adult talk. Liz wondered if Gail liked children.

At the restaurant, Liz was surprised to see the policeman who picked up Clay Markin the first day she met Gail at Maui Power.

He waved them over to his table.

From Gail's reaction, Liz surmised the meeting was prearranged.

The big guy seemed pleasant enough. Maybe Bear Huggins was Gail's contact for the police.

"Penned in their darlings, didn't they?" Gail motioned to the kids running around and then pulled out a chair next to Liz's right arm.

"I thought the bustle would hide our conversation." Bear said as the waitress handed Liz and Gail their menus. "I usually get a salad."

"A hamburger for me," Gail told the waitress, "with an extra slice of raw onion, please."

Liz could hear the strain in Bear's voice. "Are you taking every precaution?"

Gail turned a puzzled gaze away from the blonde twin toddlers. "I never disregard my overriding intuitions."

"Now, Gail…" Bear struggled to keep his dismay secret. "I fear you are too trusting."

"The waste products of one are food for the other," Gail said. "Our minds have to ignore or reject the absurd to reach transformation."

Spiritualistic jargon, the charming ignoramus before them lacked any logic, Liz concluded, and tried to let reason air. "Jung says a problem that coincides with external events, the possible murders, that contains elements of inner conflict are transformed into a question embracing the whole of society."

Bear seemed to comprehend, but Gail gave Liz a blank stare.

"He's Nero and Herod put together," Gail informed Bear.

In an attempt to explain to Liz, she added, "He asked me to perform a past-life regression."

"Halloway?" Liz and Bear said in unison and then smiled at each other over the coincidence.

"Did you know one of his fake dredging companies is called Salome?" Gail adjusted her thick glasses, motioning for the waiter to take their order.

Liz did remember Salome Dredging on letterhead in the supply room. "How do you know he was Herod?"

"He complained about Salome not returning to the palace," Gail said as a matter of fact as if she had ordered pineapple.

Bear lowered his head, presumably not to show his discomfort. "And Nero?"

"He spoke in Latin." Gail smiled at them. "And that's who Halloway said he was."

Liz didn't ask how Gail knew it was Latin. She hadn't noticed a college degree on Gail's application. Nevertheless, past-life regressions were way over Liz's head. "You believed him?"

"I'm not positive, one hundred percent." Gail fidgeted with her hair. "He could have faked it. I don't test people in those situations. It breaks down their trust."

"I see," Liz said.

She didn't, at all.

Gail bit into her giant burger. After several hearty chews, she said, "In this way,"—chomp—"the personal problem,"—swallow—"acquires a dignity it lacked before."

Cautiously, Liz tried to persuade Gail. "Begging the question of your safety alone with Halloway does not relieve an overall impression of danger."

"I know you're agitated." Gail patted Liz's arm roughly, which flipped Liz's fork laden with lettuce onto the tablecloth. "My instincts are honed to pick up sensations as fleeting as rainbows. You do have an aversion to Halloway's ugliness."

"It isn't that!" Liz tried to defend her prejudices.

This woman was reaching beyond the pale of decency.

"Tsk, tsk," Gail chirped happily.

Liz lowered her hands onto her lap, gripping them tightly. She wanted to slap this misty-eyed horror.

"I think you are mesmerized by the object of your investigation," Bear said.

Gail's expression shifted. "Halloway?"

Gail shot Liz a dubious look. "I think your privileged position could be detrimental to you."

The impudent old chit could have at it. Gail dared to attack her instead of Halloway. Fine.

"Bless your heart," Liz said in an elegiac tone. "I'm afraid you find me mettlesome in this detective affair."

Gail pushed back her hair in an irate manner. "You probably believe he's a mercenary rascal."

"We think he's linked to the man we arrested for shooting Clay's mother," Bear told her.

"Clay's mother was shot?" Gail let go of her hair,

which now contained a bit of mustard.

"Is he easy to anger?" Liz asked, knowing the answer.

"He feels exiled on his own island."

"Why is that?" Bear asked.

But Gail pointed angrily at Liz. "Her friend, high-and-mighty Svetlana, wouldn't even let Halloway see the inside of her house."

"Svetlana?" Liz asked.

Bear just looked at Liz.

"When did Halloway ask Svetlana to see it?" Liz was astonished that Gail would believe such an outright lie.

"Halloway asked her realtor," Gail said.

Liz noticed Gail's hand was shaking. "Gail, Svetlana's home is not up for sale."

"See," Gail turned this way and that, watching the children but looking unnerved.

Liz reached an arm out to comfort her.

"Don't touch me." Gail raised her voice in a fevered whine. "You condescending bitch."

Liz felt as if she had been slapped.

Mothers were scurrying the children away from their contentious table.

"I'm sorry you hold me in such contempt," Liz managed.

Gail began to sob, loudly with crude snuffs of her nose.

"Here, here, now." Bear offered his handkerchief.

Gail's entire face flowed with tears.

Finally, the storm passed.

Gail lifted her head. "I'm afraid you're right. The edges of Halloway's personality and mine are blurring.

I felt an adrenaline surge with my anger. I could be getting addicted to his rage. Please forgive any animosity I may have transported from him."

Bear patted Gail's arm, and gave her the napkin from one of the extra place settings to wipe her eyes.

"I think you're under a baleful spell," Liz said.

Gail clenched her jaw and Liz feared another outbreak of temper.

The other patrons were ogling them.

Gail resumed quietly sobbing with her head down on the table.

"I think I can take him back to a positive personality," Gail explained to Bear when she stopped crying. "Given enough time. Obstacles sometimes dam up the river of life."

"Creating swamps of hatred?" Metaphors were not Liz's strong suit either, but she didn't feel all the suspicions about Halloway's crimes should be airily swept aside.

"I know Svetlana is worried about your being alone with him."

Gail didn't have enough sense to walk across a room without a guide.

"Don't forget, he is a suspect."

"I know, but those shameful traces of hate are only one part of his potential self. Schiller says, 'Those who do not venture out beyond actuality will never capture truth.' Some dreadful hurt has inflicted a terrible wound in Halloway's soul. If I can just establish a harmony of goodness with the multiplicity of his selves, he could demonstrate any shape-shifting power."

An irrational inner reality was obviously one of Gail's dubious charms.

"Gail, I…" Liz stopped short.

Henry Halloway appeared at their table. "There you are, you little minx."

The imperious toad's brow furrowed. "What are you doing here? I still have lots of work for you."

Gail blushed, stood, and bowed in subservience.

"I was just thanking Liz for hiring me." She patted Halloway's arm as she passed by. "I enjoy working with you. You're such an interesting man."

Halloway followed Gail out of the restaurant like a lost puppy.

Liz nearly fell out of her chair.

He had averted his gaze from the policeman, Bear Huggins. If Halloway thought it was odd for Gail to lunch with a policeman and the secretary of personnel, he didn't let on.

"Chasing blatantly dangerous suspects isn't that satisfying," Bear Huggins said.

Liz looked at him. He wasn't ugly and maybe more silent than stupid. "I wish Svetlana was back."

"I wish Clay could tell Gail to quit," Bear said.

"Chris Manning showed up for work this morning," Liz told him. "Late but alive."

"Where was she?" Bear asked. "I guess that doesn't matter. Did she explain herself?"

"Gail said Chris attended her mother's funeral in Florida." Liz's nerves were on edge. She looked at the ocean's surf and then the sky. "She left a message, but our system went down that weekend."

"Captain Tanner wants me to question Halloway about Boston Commons. If Halloway asks about why we had lunch with Gail, tell him I took you both out to lunch to inquire about Chris Manning."

"Could Gail be having an affair with the creep?" Liz wasn't interested in the morality issues. She did not, could not, guarantee the woman's safety.

"She stayed with me for Christmas," Bear said, blushing adorably. "She said she was worried about the evil in Hana."

Liz had an insight. "Does Gail drink?"

Bear reluctantly nodded. "But she stays dry when she is working for Clay."

****

The thought that Halloway had always known she was a police plant didn't frighten Gail Maynard. His acrimonious remarks were second nature to him. Someone with a steam-kettle personality had to vent. The man was high-strung.

Gail asked him in front of Chris' desk. "Are you busy tonight?"

"Why are you asking for a date now that Chris has replaced you?" She noted Halloway's yellow teeth did need whitening.

Gail told herself that most people would think his way of impregnating every innocent remark with venom was criminal. She didn't feel hysterical about it. In her work as seer and investigator, bland impenetrability worked best.

"You rascal," Gail kidded, "I thought we could try another regression. There's a full moon and a lunar eclipse is predicted."

His voice slithered. "Are you thinking of doing anything disreputable with your ex-boss?"

"Not yet." Gail laughed. "Should I come over there, or cook for you?"

"Tired of my cozy place?" Halloway's tone could

only be described as malicious by those given over to mental terrors.

"I don't find your place fraught with peril," Gail lied.

She hated to cook.

"You're not really convinced of the treachery of men, are you?"

"That's ludicrous." Gail glanced toward Chris Manning and thought the woman looked like she wanted to crawl into the nearest hole.

So, Gail included her in the strange conversation. "Women are as ornery as men, aren't they, Chris?"

Chris declined any comment.

"Good," Halloway said. "Bring over Kentucky Fried. Lots of potatoes and gravy. I'm getting hungry thinking about it."

"I thought the full moon would be nice," Gail said quietly, wishing Chris could disappear again.

"Can't be detrimental." He smiled at Chris and winked an amber eye at Gail. "Come on over, get to know me better."

"Okay," Gail said, unable to move.

Thankfully, Chris excused herself. "Need to retrieve the mail," she said.

"I'll reveal all my concealed parts." Halloway's laugh was nothing less than fiendish. "Parts are parts."

Gail checked to make sure Chris was out of earshot.

Her embarrassed silence must have alerted Halloway that his crassness was way over the line of propriety.

"Don't mind my loutish peasant wit." Halloway actually apologized. "I'm looking forward to seeing you tonight."

Gail didn't hear any hatred in that statement. "Sure. See you about six."

She drove home and poured herself a stiff drink. And then another. Her nerves seemed primed for something great.

She knew Halloway would lose the last of his rancor when he met with her later.

Gail planned to wear black lace, everywhere. Stem to stern. And no bra.

Part of her seduction would be the revelation that the police now knew Halloway was innocent of all wrongdoing. That she had been their spy. The police could go jump off a cliff.

Maybe Halloway would want to join her in Australia. Start a new life after they found a past life he could emanate.

She started to pour another drink but noticed time had slipped away from her. It was time to provide chicken and gravy to the most exciting man she had ever met.

****

Halloway's anger heated to a molten fury. One of his illegitimate sons, Boston Commons, was stupid enough to shoot at Clay Markin's mom and get himself arrested in the process. Someone had given the police more information than they could possibly learn from that idiot. Gail Maynard was the only one privileged to see documents connecting himself to the Commons family. She had done more than shred what he had given her.

Extermination was the order of the day.

She'd never see that moon she was howling about.

Or maybe he should let her be snuffed out slowly, knowing her sins had infuriated the fates against her. His injurious plans didn't include patience. The devil takes the hindmost, and good riddance to traitorous females.

****

At the southern tip of Maui, in Hana, a scenario of retribution and revenge unfolded.

Gail Maynard walked a little unsteadily to Henry Halloway's house wondering at the time and interest she'd invested in the man. Did she intend to marry him with all the suspicions whirling around his reputation?

Halloway jerked open the door.

Gail imagined some romantic sorrow blighted his life. How could she be attracted to a dangerous man? His impregnable isolation abolished all relationships in his life. He'd been waiting for her.

"We're becoming gossip fodder," she said with a certain pride.

He shut the door behind her with icy care. "No one gives a damn what happens to us, much less waste a minute of their time with our antics."

With a dramatic sweep of her arm, Gail said, "You'll be free of all speculation shortly. I've cleared your name."

Halloway seemed impervious to the news.

He grabbed the arm she had swung to the fates and twisted it behind her. "Your future is unhampered."

Gail was transported.

He'd finally touched her. "A temporary accumulation of energy and its overflow into channels not used before, though lying ready, unconsciously—"

"You pious fraud," Halloway growled, his eyes

narrowing, and his face took on a hideous and unacceptable look of savagery.

Mentally confused, Gail could only return a glazed stare. She blinked, bewildered at his vehemence. Was he endeavoring to start a sexual game?

"How about a drink I've concocted just for you, you sanctimonious plague?"

Gail had heard of sadistic sexual games like this, but had never participated in any. However, with him, perhaps.

"I am the interloper here," she said, sipping a foul-smelling brown liquor. She coughed. "Your well water needs testing."

With deceptively lazy ease, Halloway seated himself on the couch in front of her.

"Should I undress?" Gail asked. "Or did you want to eat the chicken?"

"It's your funeral," he muttered.

That squelched any immediate disrobing. Gail succumbed to drowsiness too heavy to fight, and a heavy force pushed her down. She collapsed on the couch next to Halloway.

The drink was drugged, she thought. Still, she didn't panic, hoping it was part of his sexual fantasy; until a black void finally overpowered her.

****

When she awoke, she couldn't move.

It was a recurring nightmare. Only this time as she frantically tried her limbs, she found herself bound by a rope from head to toe.

Viciously loud, Halloway yelled. "Awake yet, little lady? Can you smell gasoline?"

Gail was standing on a stool. A rope was wrapped

around her neck, tied to a rafter in her own dank basement. A rag tasting of gasoline was stuffed in her mouth.

"We're about to eclipse your life." Halloway stood menacingly close. In his hands was a box of matches. "Don't stare at me as if I were a wild beast. You bloody spy."

The rope was so tight, she couldn't shake her head.

"I had my bastard sons get rid of those miserable Green Peace spies, but I saved you for myself."

All the warnings she received repeated in her brain; too late, she thought, too late.

Still, she felt great sorrow for him. She claimed a place in heaven by forgiving him.

As if he read the unwanted understanding in her eyes, Halloway shouted at her, "I'm going to burn down this cozy place with you in it, and then mine. That should clear my name of any arsons."

Halloway moved to the steps to the ground floor, gloating. "Maui's not big enough for a man like me. I'm off to Australia. Bags all packed."

He waved a ticket at her. "Got a few matches saved for my office, too."

His distorted face radiated pure hatred for her.

He lit a match and tossed it at her before he left.

Realizing her imminent fate, Gail kicked the stool out from under herself.

Her neck broke, releasing her before the flames reached the stool.

Chapter Fifteen

Thursday, December 27

Clay awoke with his arms wrapped around Svetlana.

Her dreams were causing a beatific smile. Here was his Eve reclining on green satin sheets with a backdrop of flowering trees waving their blossoms through the window. He counted the songs of twelve different morning birds. Surely, Eve had been a redhead. Svetlana's jasmine perfume lingered on the pillows. Clay noted the darker coloration of his thighs next to Svetlana's lighter skin.

Perhaps he would never have to visit Hana's tree-house motel again. Perhaps viewing Svetlana each morning would be all the refreshment his spirits would require to meet the challenges of life.

Accustomed to waking up in strange surroundings, Clay dressed quietly.

Not until he opened the door of their bedroom and stepped onto the inside balcony that circled the mammoth house, did he realize finally that this house was his new home.

This villa of wood situated on manicured grounds was designed for luxurious pleasure, from the amenities in the gorgeous limestone and glass tiled bathroom to the bamboo bedroom flooring. All of this, the handcrafted staircase, carved Chinese and Indonesian furniture, the grand piano, and original folk art—all counted as his own property.

A slight panic flipped through his stomach.

Coffee. He needed coffee to think.

Finding the kitchen and the pot, he could see Mississippi picking fresh flowers for the table from the 'ohi'a tree. She nodded with the proper prayers to appease the spirits.

Clay stole a cup of the fragrant coffee and walked in stocking feet through the dining room past the towering fireplace to the main room. The house greeted him with elegant shadows, luminous surfaces, and clean, well-rubbed smells. *His*.

A detective shouldn't live in such an elaborate setting. Clients would find the environment unseemly to bring their guilty, petty suspicions to such a noble house. They would taint the very air.

Clay found a corner of the leather couch, and stretched his long legs over the conveniently placed hassock, appreciating the ambiance of the house.

He felt a change coming on. His senses heightened as if smelling the first whiffs of a major shift in the weather, which occurred frighteningly quick on Maui.

A prisoner of his own making. That's what filling the role of divorce detective felt like. Now he was free of all that.

His mind was in a chaotic state of confusion. Clay focused his entire being in one direction: the future. His surroundings attached wings to his thoughts, carrying him he knew not where. His soul's relationship with the familiar was gone. At the collision of opposites, between his past status and this present reality, inner lacerations scoured his subterranean abode.

A home like this demanded a leader in the community as its owner, a state senator, or governor.

He thought he could find the answers, words for the encounter with his inward vision, with one more cup of coffee.

Mississippi was waiting for him in the gleaming kitchen. "Don't be ruining your stomach with all that acid."

Nevertheless, he poured himself another cup of coffee. He didn't want to speak, didn't want to break the spell of something great in the offing.

"Take a couple of these pecan rolls with you to meditate." Mississippi forced a plate and napkin into his free hand.

She seemed to guess his mind was too occupied to speak.

"I'll wait until I hear Svetlana stir to make you a tender mushroom omelet."

Clay nodded. His mind couldn't communicate yet—too much to decide.

The couch awaited his return to the fathomless depths of his soul. Sugar from the sweet roll jump-started the corners of his brain.

From disordered vague feelings, he was conscious of the reverberations of complete freedom.

Money was certainly not a limiting factor for any plan, a first for Clay Markin.

He'd have to go back to school, law school this time. While he was getting a degree, he could play around with local causes, and establish a helpful personality. Maybe become a district attorney, and build his constituency!

"Svetlana," he called from downstairs. "Svetlana, wake up."

Clay slowed his gait to regain some dignity once he hit the upstairs hallway.

He watched Mississippi shake her head at his loud foolery.

****

Wide awake from the yelling, I stretched my limbs, lifted each heel to the ceiling, then offered empty arms to my lover.

Clay kissed my mouth, pulling away from my coaxing arms.

"Don't you have to get ready for work?" he asked.

I made a cursory check of the clock. "Not at five o'clock in the morning."

Then I remembered my nightmare. "I dreamed the choking dream I had in New Mexico. A horrible yellow Mo' lizard choked me. I was the only human on the island."

Clay sat on the bed, letting me wrap my legs around his middle for comfort.

"Maui," I continued. "The god of the island looked a lot like you. He threw molten lava into the pool where the lizard was trying to drown me. The water boiled, but I miraculously felt no heat. I thought the evil Mo' had killed me."

I hugged Clay. "Then I heard Gail's lapu spirit in a smoky haze tell me that I was okay and that evil does exist."

"I'm addicted to you." Clay's arms were wrapped around me. "You are intoxicating."

"We frolic quite well together," I said. "Don't you think?"

"Pagan, that's the terms you are thinking in." Clay kissed me, scooting me to his lap. "After you're satiated."

I put up a mock struggle so that Clay would hold onto me.

"I relegate evil to non-believer property. Even though I recognize evil in myself, where does it come from?" Clay asked. "What is the ingenerate source?"

I tried to answer. "I don't know why people throw away their lives for something they think they must have."

Clay's breath tickled my ear. "Why more for them, less for everyone else when they're happiest giving?" His fingers were in my hair. "Evil always surprises us. It's out of the ordinary, disharmony."

His face was easy to read. That alone was seductive enough to instill unsteadiness in my resolve to show up for work.

What an arid and lonely life I had led.

"My heart feels too big for my chest," Clay said.

"And a mighty chest it is." I laughed and added seriously, "I love you too."

Then I disengaged myself from his tempting limbs.

Clay surprised me with, "I've got to go back to school, become a lawyer, maybe the mayor."

"Way too much coffee?" I laughed.

Clay stood and paced around the room as I disappeared into the shower.

"Listen to me," he called out. "I'm serious. What do you think? I can't be a detective in this house. What would people think?"

I peeked my head around the bathroom door. "About Senator Markin?"

196

Clay sat on the bed, calmer. "Yes."

An unusual premonition settled firmly on my shoulders. Entwined in my resonating nerves was information from another source. I rubbed my curls fiercely. What had I forgotten?

Danger.

I returned to the bedroom dressed in a light-green striped robe. "Maui would be lucky to have such a handsome leader…after our children are in school."

He smiled for all he was worth.

Then he stood, smiled, and embraced me.

Clay seemed taller than I remembered.

"How tall are you?" I asked over my shoulder as we headed down the stairs for breakfast. I had never noticed people could grow within view.

"A mile high," Clay said.

The auspicious house seemed an appropriate fit for Clay. I saw his potential, and believed in him before he did. I *did* know how to love my man.

"I feel luckier than any two men," Clay said.

He picked me up in his arms and swung me around. "Enough room to swing a canoe in," Clay laughed.

Mississippi grumbled at him. "Only one pecan roll tomorrow."

Clay kissed her ageless cheek. "It's good to be home, to have a home."

I winked at Mississippi. "All that good loving."

"Well, here is more than cool spring water." Mississippi laughed, hauling out heaping plates of omelets and bacon. "Don't flap your jaws at each other and let them get cold."

We minded her until she was safely back in the

kitchen.

"Mississippi is showing off our garden," I said.

Leis of pink and yellow plumeria encircled our plates.

"God bless Mississippi," Clay said.

I laughed. "Because she knows your appetite is as big as you."

"Hey,"—Clay reached for another roll—"my bones are twice the size of yours."

"You are a mountain of a man." I got up to kiss him again. "The first time you were in my Mustang, I wondered if the wheels would turn."

"I beg your pardon." Clay resumed devouring his morning meal.

Clay eased into Thursday's reality with each bite. "You can't go to work without me."

"That would give everything away." I felt faint, probably turned as white as a lapu ghost. "I believe if you can anticipate something, you can control it."

"What do you think is going to happen?" Mississippi joined us at the table.

That had never happened before when the house belonged to my father.

I responded to the affectionate atmosphere surrounding me. "It can't mean anything."

"I just want this dirty business over with,"— Mississippi got up to return to the kitchen—"so I can plan the wedding."

"Let's not talk about the case today." Clay stopped eating. "You're so lovely with those ruffles encircling your neck."

His compliment didn't permeate my brain or change my expression of concern. "Did they suffer, do you think?"

"If Chris Manning was killed," Clay said, "we won't give up until we find her body. I mean, try not to worry about her suffering."

"I failed them." I used my napkin to push away stray tears. "And Gail is intent on jumping off a cliff to save Halloway."

"Don't forget," Clay said, patting my hand, "Tanner is having the guy followed."

"You would think I'd feel safer with Boston Commons in jail." I tried to cheer up.

****

Clay asked Mississippi for the nearest phone in the house.

She brought him a cell phone. "Don't let those eggs get ruined."

"Yes, ma'am," Clay said, as he punched in Captain Tanner's number.

"'Bout time you got back," Tanner said. "Need you to come in and talk. When are the autopsy reports expected?"

"I've got a problem," Clay said. "Svetlana Nigel, soon to be Markin, wants to go into work, alone."

"Wow. I'll have to start talking to you like an adult, maybe," Tanner said. "Congratulations. I hope you're not neglecting the case."

"What about the stake out on Halloway?"

"We've been driving by his house, intermittently. That secretary, Gail Maynard, was at his house Christmas Eve, but she went home. Then she called Bear and then spent Christmas Day with him.

"I'm sure we've got enough evidence against Halloway for you to ask for a search warrant."

"Like what?" Tanner asked.

"Claire Nemish's folks were sent copies of his rejected real-estate offers." Clay nodded in thanks to Mississippi, who had refilled his cup. "You might want to match them with those arsons."

"Bring them in." Tanner's voice had dropped with the seriousness of the situation.

"Do you think it's safe for Svetlana to go in alone?" Clay asked.

"No. Go with her. Ask Halloway all he knows about Boston Commons."

"You finally have Boston behind bars?" Clay failed to keep the anger out of his voice.

"Sorry about your mother, Clay," Tanner said. "How is she doing?" Without waiting for a reply, he continued, "Boston is a creepy guy."

"I'll come down and question him, if you let me."

"Fine, but don't you want to tell Halloway we want to bring him in for questioning? Seems there's more than one enterprise those two have going. One is called Salome Dredging. I don't have the name for all the others, but his brother owns that salvage dump the VIN was traced to. Can't figure out any connection to Maui Power."

"I'll catch up with Svetlana later in the day," Clay said. "We found purchase orders to a Salome Dredging." Clay was getting excited. They were close to shutting Halloway behind bars. "Could be for around half a million dollars." Then Clay remembered to ask, "Anything about Chris Manning?"

"Nothing, just seemed to vanish," Tanner added. "After you question Boston Commons, we'll visit the DA together, okay?"

Mississippi patted Clay's back as she went by to answer the front doorbell.

"Tennessee!" Clay heard Mississippi shout and then started sobbing. "Come on in."

"I'll be right over." Clay ended his call.

Clay's chair faced the main door. Kani Nigel and Clay's mother entered the dining room.

He rose and embraced his mother, holding her for a minute more than was necessary for a normal greeting. He was sorry for all the years they were separated by a misunderstanding.

"Good to see you both," he added. "Svetlana's upstairs."

Clay offered Kani his chair.

"You finished already?" Kani declined the offer, taking a seat, instead, in the middle of the table. "Mississippi, am I allowed to enjoy one of your omelets this morning?"

"No trouble at all," Mississippi said.

"Join us, Mother," Clay said, reseating himself to keep them company.

"How's the case coming?" She stood behind Kani's chair with her hand on his shoulder.

"The secretary-detective I recommended to shake out facts from Halloway…"—Clay hesitated—"seems to be interested in his nicer side."

Clay got up from the table, feeling more like pacing than sitting. "Gail is doing a series of past-life regressions for Halloway, to gain his confidence."

"Hypnotizing someone to get the truth of them could be dangerous." Tennessee moved uncomfortably behind Kani's chair.

"Are you in pain?" Kani asked.

"I'm curious to see the house," Tennessee said. "I haven't been here since Karen's funeral. I'll just run up and chat with my new daughter-in-law."

Mississippi called after her, "I'll be making you a cheese and mushroom omelet so you hurry back down here.'

"I know that's not a textbook police method." Clay wasn't happy to be left to appease the old bird sitting at the table. "The police asked me to meet with the District Attorney this afternoon."

Deciding to go on the offensive, Clay said, "I'm sure you'll take good care of my mother."

Kani didn't answer the implied question. "Sure seems odd with you sitting at the head of the table when we came in."

Clay felt thoroughly embarrassed. "Mississippi insisted."

"She was right." Kani actually smiled. "It just felt odd. I was lonesome living here after Svetlana went off to school."

"I didn't know you were interested in my mother."

"For fifteen years," Kani said. "Even longer, if the truth were something to talk about." Kani began to pace the room, looking up the stairwell after the women. "Your mother was a tough nut to crack. Sorry. But she said she did miss me all those years. That helped a little."

Clay was at a loss for words, so he repeated himself, "Mother will be well taken care of."

"But will I make her happy?" Kani asked. "That's what I ask myself about you and my daughter." Kani resumed his seat. "Will she be happy?"

How did the shoe get on the other foot. "Svetlana

agrees that I should go back to school to become a lawyer, get into politics."

"Really?" Kani asked, in what Clay thought was a satirical tone.

Clay's back was to the staircase, but he knew Svetlana was joining them by the comforting fragrance of jasmine.

Kani smiled confidently at Clay. "I think the giant has fallen for you, Svetlana."

Tennessee followed Svetlana down the stairs. She reached for Kani's hands. "They're planning for us to be grandparents, more than once."

"I found out Clay's going into politics," Kani said, "if I pay his way to law school."

Clay tensed. He never asked such a thing but figured this was Kani's way to show his approval of that decision.

Tennessee came over and hugged Clay.

"I'm hoping you don't blame me for your injury," Clay said softly.

"Oh,"—Tennessee laughed—"Was it you that shot me? I thought you and Svetlana were on the mainland collecting evidence."

"We should be going." Kani rubbed his hands over the closed keyboard of the grand piano. "Svetlana should play for you one day, Clay."

"Karen loved that piano," Tennessee explained to Clay.

"I promise," Svetlana kissed Clay's mother goodbye. "I feel as if I'm getting my mother back."

That was odd; Clay felt he was losing Tennessee all over again.

After they left, Svetlana shook her head. "I feel about fifteen again."

"Me too," Clay said, hugging her to his chest.

Chapter Sixteen

After Svetlana left for work, Mississippi was in a chatty mood. "Liked you the first time I laid eyes on you, Clay Markin."

She started to clear the table. "My boy Bear keeps me posted on your shenanigans. This wedding is going to tip the scales."

Clay laughed. "I've got to live through meeting the Rutledge family members."

"Those folks? Nothing to be afraid of." Mississippi patted the top of his head as she poured him another cup of coffee. "I've changed diapers on most of them."

"Well, that will keep me cheerful if they get too high and mighty."

"That's right." Mississippi was in rare form. "And the most important thing to remember is that you are a happy man. They're still looking for bliss. You can tie your kite to any dream, big Maui man like you."

"You suppose Bear can stand up for me as my best man?"

"If he says maybe,"—Mississippi stood with her arms akimbo—"You tell him his ma wants to talk to him."

Clay enjoyed having his own rah-rah-rah team at home. "I'm glad you decided to stay with the house," he said, kissing her weathered cheek.

"Have to bury me out back somewheres."

Mississippi laughed loudly.

Clay thought he might have embarrassed Mississippi slightly.

Svetlana promised to call when she got to work. How long did that take?

He excused himself and returned upstairs to dress for his trip to the police station.

His white silk suit did not tempt him. Instead, he chose jeans and a T-shirt. The morning spent questioning Boston Commons would require releasing the dragon of anger within himself. Instead of sandals, he wore his stomping boots.

Pocketing his cell phone, Clay let the MG full out to speed to the police station in Wahikuli.

Captain Tanner escorted him directly to the examining room. "Isn't eight o'clock a bit early for an almost newlywed?" he teased.

"We need to shut down Halloway," Clay said. "Boston Commons is the key."

The kid was not good-looking by any means possible.

"How old are you?" Clay asked the scroungy guy with genuine curiosity.

"What difference does that make?" Boston was sullen. His hair was thinning, and his teeth looked old, yellowed from coffee, Clay guessed.

"I want to know how old a fool has to be to mistake me for my mother." Clay sat across the metal table from the handcuffed man.

"Didn't shoot anyone," he said.

"Did I say my mother was shot?" Clay looked at Tanner, who was sitting in the room on the other side of the two-way mirror.

"He promised me a lawyer," Boston grumbled into the neck of his dirty shirt, "if I got in trouble."

His chin almost touched his chest.

"Look at me!" Clay shouted. "Do you see a lawyer in here?"

Clay made a sport of standing and pacing to unnerve a suspect in the green-painted concrete block walled room. Then he sat down and bent to look under the table.

"Any lawyers hiding under here?"

"No." Boston stared straight at Clay, looking scared.

"Who is he?" Clay asked more quietly.

"He'll see that I'm killed. Can you uncuff me?"

Clay hesitated, staring the kid down before unlocking the handcuffs.

Boston tugged his hair at the back of his neck. "Don't let any of my bastard brothers in to visit me, either." He rubbed his wet palms on his dirty jeans. "He's got enough money to buy anybody."

"So he paid you to shoot my mother," Clay said.

Without thinking of the consequences, Boston said, "Not yet."

Clay didn't bother looking toward Tanner listening in the other room. "Ever work for him before?"

"Got to, Ma said." Boston looked around the room expecting The Man from Chi or Chicken Little to announce the sky was falling.

"All you boys work for your father?" Why else would all the kids do what their mother told them?

"Bastard. Never married Ma." Boston's nose turned red. "He supports us all, one way or another."

Clay's anger seeped away. "How many brothers do

you have?"

Boston pulled out an unclean wad of a rag. "Vegas, Phoenix, Austin, Houston, Dallas." He wiped at his nose and eyes. "Jackson, Nixon, and Ralston."

Clay carefully wrote down each name in his evidence notebook. Then he asked in a conversational tone, "Now, why did you say he had you tail Svetlana Nigel?"

"Oh, she was making such a fuss about the girls' accident." Boston squirmed as if vermin were possibly residing in his clothing. "He thought Svetlana might find something on him, working in personnel and all."

Clay stared at him, waiting for more.

He patted his pocket, and took out his cell phone to check that it was on and charged.

Why hadn't she called?

Boston moved nervously in his chair. "Now you just wait a minute. I seen on a police TV program that if you get me a lawyer, he can make a deal so's I wouldn't have to stay in jail. Maybe be put in protective custody on the mainland away from Ma."

"Now you're thinking like a grown man," Clay said. "You'd tell us who your boss is? Cooperate?"

"Yeah, that's the word," Boston said. "Then I get immunity for everything we boys did."

Clay heard a knock on the glass mirror. "Wait here a minute."

Captain Tanner was still on the phone when he entered the other room. "Clay, Fire Inspector just called. Last night there were two fires in Hana. One at Halloway's house and one at Gail's."

"Oh, shit!" Clay said. "Better head down there."

As they hurried out of the adjacent room, Clay

glanced at Boston on the other side of the window. The man was letting himself go, body shaking, head on his crossed arms, weeping. Clay empathized with his misery…for a moment.

Tanner hit Clay's upper arm. "He's just sorry he got caught."

"Do you have enough men to pick up the rest of the eight brothers?"

"No problem," Tanner said. "I'll send Bear down to Hana."

Clay remembered the unnamed father. "Do you think that kid looks like he could be Halloway's illegitimate son?"

"Ugly enough," Tanner said. "I didn't even know eyebrows could slant down like that. Hard to make a happy face with that mug."

In any other mood, Clay might have enjoyed the joke. "Better keep those boys separated until we figure out which one of them torched the houses."

"Might as well bring in their mother, too." Tanner put his hand on Clay's arm, again. "Wait, Clay, you need to know this," Tanner said. "Bear went to lunch with Gail and Liz Cameron yesterday. Gail said she was in love with Halloway."

"Yeah," Clay said. "Gail told me when I gave her a ticket to return to Australia."

Tanner stepped in front of him, too close.

Clay explained in detail. "I had to clear the decks before I had dinner with Svetlana's father. Gail said she'd have to visit Halloway in jail."

"That ditz said she was in love with Halloway?" Tanner had not moved from blocking Clay's retreat down the hall from the jail's examining room.

"You know, Bear's been sweet on Gail for years."

"Didn't know that," Tanner said.

"What about the district attorney?" Clay asked.

"He said to be there at eight-thirty. We need you to run through the case." Tanner finally stepped aside for Clay. "I'll send Horowitz to Hana instead of Bear."

"Penelope Windgate might want to search the place," Clay suggested.

****

Clay's worry about Svetlana and Gail Maynard's safety took a back seat when they assembled at the district attorney's office.

The library conference room of the law office mimicked courtroom paneling where the law books didn't reach the ceiling. The chairs were as hard as the jury section. Clay thought he could smell the glue in the books; maybe the leather covers gave off the odor.

"Get comfortable,"

Bear left for Hana without so much as a goodbye.

Clay wished he could drop the boxes and run over to Maui Power. His steel nerves upped his anxiety. Why hadn't Svetlana called him yet?

Roy Jaffee told Tanner as if they enjoyed a private joke.

"We don't plan to stay long." Tanner opened the door. "Bear, bring those boxes in here."

"What's this?"

"Evidence of provable embezzlement, a trail of arson, and two, possibly three, murders," Tanner said grandly. "This is Clay Markin. His fiancée is Svetlana Nigel. They hired Gail Maynard to act as Henry Halloway's secretary. Gail collected most of this for you. By the way, Gail's house in Hana was torched last night."

Bear stopped in the doorway with his arms laden with the third stack of records.

Clay understood his quandary. He stepped over to Bear to help him with the boxes.

"Captain Tanner," Clay said when he saw the pain in Bear's eyes. "I think Bear needs to head for Hana."

"What?" Tanner turned and sized up the situation. "Right. Bear, you better see that Miss Windgate follows the rules."

Bear left for Hana without so much as a goodbye.

Clay wished he could drop the boxes and run over to Maui Power. His steel nerves upped his anxiety. Why hadn't Svetlana called him yet?

Clay forced himself to return to the subject at hand. "Penelope Windgate gave us her preliminary notes about two of the murder victims. The bodies of Claire Nemish and Pam O'Brian were found on Sunday, December 9th in the remains of a salvaged vehicle that was pushed over the side of Haleakala Highway. We traced the VIN to Vegas Commons."

"Mr. Jaffee," Captain Tanner concluded, "after the autopsy reports arrive from the mainland of the exhumed bodies, we should find fibers and other clues about where Henry Halloway might have had the young women killed before they were placed in the wreck."

"Another young woman, Chris Manning, who also worked for Halloway went missing after only three days on the job." Clay wanted to be sure the record was set straight. "Svetlana Nigel came to me to help solve her suspicions about Halloway's involvement in the deaths of Pam and Claire, and possibly Chris. We need a warrant to search his car, office, bank accounts, and computers; as well as the ruins of his home in Hana that was also set on fire last night, possibly to hide evidence. We need warrants for each of the Commons' brothers' domiciles, too."

"Halloway's name did come up in the ongoing arson investigations." Jaffee called in his staff of three lawyers. "How many Commons boys are there?"

"Nine." Clay ripped out the page of his notebook with their list of names and handed it to Jaffee.

Jaffee's secretary brought in donuts and coffee.

"We plan to bring the whole family in for questioning," Tanner said, "including their mother."

Clay helped himself to two donuts.

If these young lawyers knew what they were doing, Halloway would be behind bars awaiting trial in no time. "We think the Commons boys are illegitimate sons of Henry Halloway."

"We do?" Captain Tanner asked. "They look alike."

"DNA can prove any family connection," Jaffee said.

In case they missed the point the first time, Clay repeated, "The two girls were dead before they were placed in the car, according to Penelope Windgate." Clay added for the younger lawyers, who might not have had contact with her, "the Maui Medical Examiner."

Jaffee turned to Tanner.

Tanner pointed to the boxes Bear had dumped in the room. "In there."

"Both girls sent their parents on the mainland incriminating evidence against Halloway," Clay said. "We think Halloway found out about the shipments of documents and had them killed."

"What kind of evidence?" the brown-eyed lawyer with too much curly hair over his ears asked.

"Purchase orders to bogus companies," Tanner explained. "One of them is Salome Dredging."

"Boston Commons ran that." The lady lawyer crossed her legs. "Tanner's got him in jail for attempted homicide."

"Shot my mother," Clay said. "She was getting into my car in her garage."

After a subdued silence, Clay reassured them, "She's okay."

"Wait a minute." The third man on the team held up his hand. "Are you claiming Henry Halloway, the Purchasing Director of Maui Power, murdered two women because they stole copies of purchase orders? What, to bogus companies? Why would he want to embezzle funds?"

"Svetlana and I visited both sets of parents of the young women." Clay was getting restless.

For one thing, Clay hated repeating himself. He hoped Tanner was not wasting his time with Jaffee. Clay stomped around the conference table, his boots echoing in the high ceiling. The room suddenly seemed smaller than Tanner's investigation room.

"Claire Nemish sent home rejected real estate offers of Halloway's. I think the purchase orders to Salome Dredging company funneled money through the Commons family back to Halloway. Over half a million dollars."

"Couldn't afford to buy the house he wanted on Maui," Tanner added. "According to my officer, Bear Huggins, who heard it from Gail Maynard herself."

"Impossible," Jaffee said with skepticism. "People don't steal and kill people to buy prime property."

The room remained silent.

"Crazies might," the brown-eyed kid said.

"I don't really care why the asshole did it," Tanner grimaced at his own language. "Sorry. You already admitted Halloway is suspected of having houses torched when the owners turned him down. We have his rejected offers for most of the houses on Maui. Now he's killing people to cover up his bank-rolling schemes to make bigger offers. Those two girls were just the beginning. Now the spy Clay and Svetlana hired has had her house burned to the ground. We still can't find the body of Chris Manning."

"Tanner, I'll get you all the search warrants you need." Jaffee waved his crew out of the room.

"She might have alerted him," Tanner said. He winced. "Bear Huggins told me on Wednesday that Gail Maynard was in love with Halloway."

"Nevertheless," Jaffee said. "The motive stands."

As Jaffee laid his hand on the conference room door, the phone rang.

He handed the phone to Tanner. "It's for you, Captain."

Chapter Seventeen

I had to admit, I was a little weak in the knees before I arrived at Maui Power Thursday morning.

Liz Cameron met me outside the Personnel Office door. "We have lots of surprises for you inside."

I smiled, expecting a shower of gifts and flowers, best wishes for my wedding.

I smoothed my skirt, hoping my jacket hid the few wrinkles from the drive down. However, Liz did not know I proposed to Clay. Or did he propose to me? Maybe my father squared the deal. I quit smiling when I pondered the puzzle.

Liz reacted to the change in my mood. "Now don't get impatient. This is good news." She swung the door to her office open.

"Did you hear that Clay's mother was shot by the guy that was tailing me?" I asked.

"Is she okay?"

"She's mending nicely. The police arrested the guy, Boston Commons."

"Why was he tailing you?" Liz sat at her desk. "Shooting Clay's mother?"

"We think he's connected to Halloway," I said, moving toward my door.

Liz jumped between the door and me.

"Wait," she said. "You gave me a start with your dreadful news. But everything is okay now. She came in for a minute on Wednesday directly from the plane but she looked so tired, I told her to go home."

Liz moved aside as I opened the doors to my inner office. "I said if she came in this morning, she could explain directly to you."

Chris Manning stood up from my blue couch.

Never was I as glad to see a person. "Alive!" I said.

Chris clutched one of my yellow pillows to her chest, startled by my enthusiasm.

She stepped back but I forged forward. I gratefully embraced my pillow and her plump body.

"Thank God you are safe." I breathed in her cheap lilac perfume. No one ever smelled as good.

At least I had not failed to protect one of the secretaries from Halloway.

I let the struggling girl go.

"We were so worried." I tried to explain my warm greeting. "We even went to your apartment to look for you."

"My mother died in Florida," Chris said. "I left a message on your machine."

"Did you get our note?" I asked.

"Yeah," Chris drawled, replacing my pillow correctly on the blue couch.

"The place was a mess." Chris didn't look pleased. "Yellow tape on the outside, white powder everywhere. If my landlady wasn't so busy with her own mother, she would probably have boxed up my things and rented the place right out from under me."

"Does Captain Tanner know you're safe?" I asked. I needed to call Clay on his cell phone. I smiled at the girls.

"Who's he?" Chris asked Liz.

My head started spinning. I went behind my desk, seeking the familiar comfort of my executive chair.

"Sit down, you two." I motioned for them to occupy the chairs across from my desk as I dialed Captain Tanner's office.

"I phoned my old desk in Purchasing on Wednesday,"—Chris twisted her hands—"because the police wouldn't believe me."

I hung up my desk phone. Then I looked at my hands. They were shaking.

"Who answered?" I asked.

I spread my hands, palm down on the cool glass top of my desk. I was experiencing a certain apprehension.

"That I was who I said I was," Chris continued. "They wanted me to come in. But I was so mad that they messed up my place and they wouldn't believe me. Gail answered. She doesn't like you, by the way."

"Oh," I said, hurt somehow. Even if I thought Gail was flaky, she didn't have to dislike me in return. "I hired Gail to spy on Henry Halloway."

"Yeah. Gail said you wanted to hang my murder on Halloway."

"We were worried," I tried to explain. "Remember, you replaced the two young women who died the Sunday before I hired you."

"That was an accident," Chris dismissed.

"Not according to the Medical Examiner," I said. "They were murdered before they were shoved in that wreck that was pushed over the cliff. The VIN came from a car owned by a salvage company." I reached for the phone again. "Captain Tanner, please. This is Svetlana Nigel."

Chris whimpered. "Are they going to arrest me?"

I smiled at the silly girl. "No, dear, they're going to protect you. Tanner?" I asked the dispatcher. "How about Clay Markin?" While I waited, I looked at Liz. "Where's Gail?" Once the dispatcher started to speak, I motioned for one second with my finger to Liz. "Okay. Try to reach them at the DA's office."

"Kind of late this morning, even for her," Liz admitted. "She knows Chris is back. They talked on Wednesday."

"Stay on the line," I uncharacteristically raised my voice. "Wait," I said, apologizing to the dispatcher. "I need to give you a message."

"Gail knows Chris is here," Liz repeated.

"You said that." I almost ended my call, but Liz got agitated.

"Gail's in love with Halloway," Liz said.

Chris nodded her head as if she knew that too.

"Bear was with us for lunch," Liz said. "Gail told us she was in love with Halloway."

"You're saying she might have told Halloway that Chris was alive?" My head almost grasped the danger, but not quite until Liz confirmed my fears.

"Gail might have told Halloway she was spying for you,"—Liz couldn't sit still any longer—"and she's not here."

Discouraged and frightened by this new revelation, I turned back to the call. "Tell Captain Tanner. No. Get someone over to the DA's. Do not wait for them to return. Tell Tanner and Clay Markin that Gail is missing and may have disclosed to the suspect, Henry Halloway, that she was an undercover agent for the police."

I hung up the phone. Maybe I should try Clay's cell?

Chris stood up, too, as if to leave my office.

"Oh no," I said. "Liz, keep Chris in my office and lock your outer door. The police will explain when they get here. Clay Markin wears a white silk suit. You'll be able to identify him through the door's glass side panel. Only let him in."

"Where are you going?" Chris began to cry when I got up to leave my office.

"I just want to make sure Gail is not at her desk." I slipped my cell phone into one pocket and the small gun Clay's mother provided me into the other pocket of my jacket. "I'll be right back."

"Why don't I go with you?" Liz asked.

"I need you to keep Chris safe," I said. "I know I can count on you."

Liz locked the door behind me.

I made the trip up the marble staircase with little trepidation. As soon as I found Gail, I'd phone Clay, even if he was in the DA's office.

Gail's desk was empty. Maybe, with Chris' safe return, she didn't feel the need to come in. I hoped.

Halloway was absent also, but it was only eight-thirty-five. He usually showed up at nine.

I waited out back in the parking lot for Gail to keep her from any harm.

Henry Halloway arrived before Gail. He spotted me.

With some hesitation, I approached him. Clay and Tanner knew there might be trouble. They were probably minutes away. Halloway would not harm me in broad daylight.

"Gail is late for work," I said as nonchalantly as possible.

Halloway ducked his head, avoiding eye contact. "That's unusual. Wait. I think she had a doctor's appointment."

"Oh," I said, recoiling as he came near. I would never get used to the rancid smell of his hair gel. "I need to talk to her."

"About Chris Manning returning?"

"Who told you?" I was shocked, and right then I knew I was in trouble.

"Gail maintains a veneer of respect." Halloway stood in front of me, his car directly behind me. "She never revealed her animosities toward me, like you have."

Panic, anxiety, name it, flooded my veins.

I tried to walk back to the office, but he blocked my way. There were no windows on the backside of the Maui Power's office building. No one would be the wiser if I were in danger.

Trying to placate him, I said. "I'm sorry if my coldness has offended you. I try to maintain a professional distance."

"Proximity is not a problem for you?" Halloway took a step closer and put his left hand on his car next to my hip. He unlocked the trunk of the Lincoln with his right, and I spotted the luggage.

I didn't move. Fear had immobilized me, but the thought of another woman missing infuriated me. "You know where Gail is."

"She's maneuvered herself into a calamity," he said, his features growing menacingly darker. No, evil-looking.

I lifted my chin to look him in the eye. "I want to see her, now."

"No problem," he said, and tried to push me into his trunk.

Before I could react, Halloway had his meaty hands around my neck, choking me. I stammered out, "The police a-are com…ing."

I must have lost consciousness because I woke up lying on the parking lot gravel. Halloway was placing the luggage from the trunk to the back seat.

A moan escaped my lips while trying to get up because Halloway stopped and leered down at me. As though I was nothing more than a rag doll, he picked me up and shoved me into the trunk.

Chapter Eighteen

Tanner accepted the phone impatiently. His eyes narrowed, ready to chew out the ear of whoever thought it was necessary to interrupt his meeting with the district attorney.

He turned his back to the conference table, walking a few steps away. With the first words spoken to him during the call, his body stiffened.

Tanner spun around to address Clay. "Mrs. Markin is in trouble. Not your mother. Svetlana!"

"Where is she?" Clay rose, and his chair toppled backward by the force.

"According to the dispatcher," Tanner said, "Svetlana called from Maui Power's office. Gail is late for work and Chris Manning showed up."

Clay paid no attention to the whereabouts of Gail and Chris. Only one woman's safety concerned him. "Why did you say Svetlana was in trouble?"

"We lost track of Halloway last night, after the fire." Tanner's voice cracked with unprofessional emotion.

Clay took out his cell and dialed Svetlana's office number. "Liz, this is Clay."

"Gail knows Chris is okay," Liz said in a rush. "But Gail hasn't shown up yet. Svetlana went to her office to see if she arrived earlier, but it's been fifteen minutes and she's not back yet."

Clay told Liz to stay in her office with Chris, with the door locked. "Bear Huggins and I will be there shortly. When Svetlana returns, tell her to stay in the office with you two."

"Clay," Liz said, "could she have driven to Hana to find Gail?"

"I'm on my way to Maui Power," Clay said then hung up. Tanner blocked his way to the door. "I think she is okay," Clay said. "But I've got to get to her before Halloway does."

"Why didn't Gail inform the police that Chris Manning was no longer missing?" Jaffee asked.

Clay ignored the District Attorney's question.

"We don't know," Tanner said. "The problem is Gail probably told Halloway that Chris is okay and then revealed she was our spy."

Clay pushed past Tanner and exited.

"Not healthy," Jaffee said. "Why would she put herself in jeopardy?"

"Seems she misunderstood danger," Tanner said,

For a split second, Clay stopped in the carpeted hall outside the conference room to hear Tanner finish his statement.

"…for excitement of a more personal nature," Tanner concluded.

On the way down to Maui Power, Clay wished Bear was with him or at least following with the police car's siren blaring.

Clay didn't slow his MG down. His speedometer hit 70 miles per hour on one curve. He kept to the incline by down-shifting and flooring the gas. He could hear the squeal of the tires.

Another squad car flashed his lights and sounded

his siren to pull Clay over.

"Yes. I'm speeding." Clay laughed, hoping whoever was following wouldn't shoot out his tires. He ignored them. Hands clutched the wheel, eyes on the road. His only thought was to get to Svetlana before Halloway harmed her or anyone else.

At Maui Power, Clay jumped out of the car, flinging the cop a signal to follow as he ran to the building.

Then he yelled back, "Radio for more help. People may be in danger inside."

Clay's anguish rose as he pounded on Svetlana's office door. A scared, heavy-set young woman looked out the side panel, then stepped behind the door.

"Let me in. I'm Clay Markin."

She was crying. "Where's your white suit?"

"I didn't wear it," Clay yelled. "Damn it, let me in."

"No. Liz said not to."

The cop, a young kid Clay didn't recognize, sauntered up behind him. "I radioed for help. What's the problem?"

"Liz is not in there?" Clay was still yelling.

"No," Chris yelled back. "She went up to Gail's office about a half-hour ago."

Clay motioned for the cop to come within view. "Here's a police officer, Chris. Let him in."

Clay read the kid's badge, "Jimmy, stay with this young woman. She may be in danger."

He heard the office door unlock as he raced up the marble steps.

"Oh, God," he prayed, "don't let Svetlana be harmed."

Out of context, but relevant to the situation, Clay remembered Svetlana's nightmares of being choked.

No one was around the Purchasing Department.

The doors were locked. Clay kicked them in, one at a time.

The rooms were empty.

"Svetlana," he called, like an idiot. "Svetlana, Liz!"

Clay ran back down the steps and called to the cop, "Is Chris okay?"

"Yes."

"Call Captain Tanner. Tell him Svetlana is still missing, and her secretary, Liz Cameron, can't be found."

Just then, Liz ran into the foyer of Maui Power. "Svetlana's car is still here."

"Go stay with Chris, Liz." Clay ran to his MG. "I'm going over to Halloway's in Hana."

"I'll follow you." Jimmy held the main door open for him.

"Sure," Clay yelled. "We'll need all the help we can get."

Fifteen minutes down the road, Clay saw the squad car in his rear-view mirror. He had turned on his emergency lights and siren again.

Ahead of him, Clay could see smoke still rising from the ruins at Halloway's and Gail's addresses in Hana.

****

"Ten o'clock." That was the time Tanner quoted when I dialed 911 on my cell phone from the trunk of Henry Halloway's car. The idiot, thankfully, hadn't thought to grab my phone.

I had been unconscious for nearly two hours.

Clay must be frantic.

I finally got through to Tanner and he asked if I was injured.

I tasted the blood on my fingertips after exploring the huge bump on my head.

"I'm in the trunk. My head is bleeding and my throat hurts," I whispered, afraid Halloway might hear me. "Halloway told me he was going to take me to Gail. The car is moving."

I remembered Clay wanted to hear from me every half-hour. "Should I hang up and call Clay?"

"No," Tanner said hurriedly. "Clay and Bear are on the road looking for Halloway's car. Let's concentrate on getting you out of that trunk."

The roof of the trunk radiated heat. The air inside was stuffy, making each intake of breath harder.

The lingering odors from the leather luggage mixed with the fumes from the carpet or the exhaust irritated my nose and eyes. In my prone position, I struggled clumsily to take off my jacket. I removed the gun that Clay's mother insisted I take for my protection from one of the jacket's pockets.

I realized the peril I was in. Halloway would have to be shot if I wanted to stay alive.

I bundled my jacket for a pillow and bandage under my aching head. I wanted to weep, but that would only make me more helpless.

My usual haughty, disdainful attitude was useless now.

The loud noises of passing cars and the bumpy ride rattled my nerves. Where the hell was he taking me?

I remembered looking up at Halloway and trying to block the blow. He had hit me with a tire iron.

"Halloway may think I'm dead," I told Captain Tanner.

"Let's keep it that way," Tanner said. "At least until we locate you and figure a way to get you out of there."

Halloway was making plans for the disposal of my body. That had to be it. Somewhere out of the way.

I tried to keep calm and viewed with contempt all my warnings to Gail to be careful. I had been just as blissfully unaware of my own vulnerability.

At least I had a loaded gun.

How could I fend Halloway off once he stopped the car? My courage faltered, draining my strength. Hopefully, I would have a chance to ask for Gail's forgiveness in judging her as reckless. With all too glaring clarity, I could see I acted just as impulsively as Gail.

The man Gail thought she loved, Henry Halloway's deviltry knew no bounds.

****

Clay stood by the blackened front steps of Gail's house. He beat his forehead with his fist. He thought he could smell Svetlana's jasmine perfume on his hands. His body felt numb, rigid with shock.

Bear was talking to Penelope Windgate. Clay watched the six-foot-eight cop kind of collapse into himself.

Clay ambled toward them, each step a burden, heavy and slow.

"Clay." Penelope straightened from talking to Bear, who was hunkered down on his ankles now, bent over with grief. "They found Gail's body."

Clay helped Bear stand. "Body?"

"She hung herself." Bear turned to Clay, his face chalked with the trauma of Gail's death.

"No, she didn't," Clay said with certainty. "She had a ticket to Australia. She was looking forward to the case ending. No way would she kill herself."

"She was dead before the fire touched her," Penelope said. "She must have kicked over the stool she was standing on. But you could be right. Maybe Gail chose an easier death than being burned alive. There was a gasoline-soaked rag in her mouth."

Bear turned his back and vomited.

"She was killed, Bear." Clay helped his friend to the patrol car. "We have to find Svetlana before Halloway kills her too.

Penelope Windgate answered her cell. "It's Tanner. "He wants to talk to you."

Nothing mattered anymore; the world was empty without Svetlana. Why had he rejected her those few hours they were together on the mainland when his arms could have been locked securely around her?

If Halloway had hurt her, maybe even…

Clay could hear Tanner yelling at Penelope, who was holding the phone away from her face. "Tell that man to come to the phone."

That man. What kind of a man would let his future wife go off to work when he knew she had to deal with a maniac?

Clay grabbed the phone. "What?" he yelled.

"Svetlana called."

"Where is she?" Clay's nerves were about to explode.

"She's in Halloway's trunk."

"Where is his car?"

"We'll find it," Tanner said. "Send Bear up the east road toward Lahaina. You take the west one. I'm staying here with her on the line."

"Let me talk to her."

"Get going!"

Clay gave Bear Penelope's phone. "Do you know what kind of a car Halloway drives?"

"A maroon Lincoln." Bear handed him a two-way radio. "Take this. We'll find her."

****

I could tell Tanner did not want to panic me. Intuitively, I knew he was withholding information about Gail.

"Do you have your purse?" Tanner asked. "A nail file, anything sharp?"

"I have a small gun."

"Good." He sounded overly relieved. "Now, search around you. A tire iron? A screwdriver handy?"

He couldn't possibly know what direction Halloway was going. Clay and Bear needed to find Halloway's car quickly.

"My ears just popped," I whispered.

"Okay. Altitude. That means he's taking you up to the volcano. We'll get there, Svetlana," Tanner said, and I prayed he was right.

I heard Tanner tell the dispatcher, "Tell Clay and Bear, that Halloway is headed for the Haleakala Crater." After a short pause, he said, "Find anything?"

"Clean as a whistle in here," I said. "Would my high-heel work?"

"Maybe. I want you to try and pop the trunk before he stops the car."

"Won't he hear me?"

229

"Svetlana, you've got to get out of there. When you hear a car pass, pound on the lock, or try to pry it open."

I sniffled. Anxiety pinged through me.

"Shit," he said. "Don't cry. Svetlana, you can do it. Help is on the way."

"I have to lay the phone down," I said.

"Leave it on, Svetlana." Tanner panicked, from his tone of voice.

I knew enough not to shut it off.

"Okay," I said.

I wiped away the warm blood running down my face, close to my ear. I laid down the phone next to the gun and worked on pulling the lock out with the stiletto heel of my shoe.

****

Henry Halloway had to admit his plan was vague.

"Those bunglers," he said aloud.

On this small island, all the Maui police would still have their hands in their pockets, after he'd escaped to Australia.

With merciless coldness, he patted the tire iron next to him. He'd taken it out of the trunk to give the slumped body of Svetlana one more good rap before throwing her into the trunk and slamming the lid.

Halloway gave an obnoxious chortle. He liked doling out judgments to those who violently opposed him.

Gail was too stupid to keep her mouth shut.

Too bad Boston Commons wasn't out on the street. A miraculous pratfall into a handy grave would have served Boston just as well as jail. Maybe he should visit the quarrelsome youth. Take a box of brandied chocolates, laced for eternity.

He hated all his offspring. Thankfully, he hadn't married their stupid mother, or the police would have linked Halloway to the arsons by now.

Halloway looked at his watch. Noon. No wonder his stomach was growling.

He drove into a roadside shop, and then pounded on the trunk, listening.

"All quiet," he told himself. Time enough to grab a bite. It was going to be a long day.

He would have to wait for dark to dump the body.

His plane didn't leave until 6:00 am.

Plenty of time.

****

A loud thud on the trunk startled me, and my shoe tumbled. What felt like days of working on the lock to open it, failed.

The distinct jingle of keys somewhere outside caught my attention. Dear God, he's going to open the trunk. Think, Svetlana, think. I placed my body in a fetal position, carefully holding and hiding the gun against my chest. My eyes shut, and I prayed my body wasn't trembling as I thought it was. Just as the slightest stream of light came through as the trunk was being lifted, I took a deep breath and prayed.

"Stupid kids. Couldn't get anything right."

Halloway's voice sounded close. The stench of meat and beer hit my nostrils as his breath blew by my face. My fingers tightened around the gun's handle. I was caked with anxiety.

"I'll be long gone by the time they find your body." His voice resonated no remorse, just pure evil. How could Gail not have picked up on that? Was love totally blind, as they say? Without meaning to, I forgot I was playing dead when I took a deep breath.

"What the—" I heard Halloway mumble, and he slammed a fist against my already aching shoulder.

My eyes opened, but everything was blurry from the tears streaming down. I did my best and launched onto my back, gun pointed at him, hands trembling.

"What're you gonna do, shoot me?" He laughed. He actually laughed.

In one quick movement, while distracted by his egotistical mirth, he grabbed my hand and took the gun. "What does it take to kill you?"

"You're not going to kill her, Halloway," came a familiar voice nearby. "Put the weapon down, put your hands up, and walk back from the car."

Bear. Oh my God, Bear was here.

Time seemed to slow at that point. Halloway's eyes narrowed, and I watched as he aimed my gun right at me.

All I could think about at that moment was never seeing Clay, my dad, or Tennessee again. I raised my gun and aimed at Halloway.

An explosive bang rang out.

Chapter Nineteen

Captain Tanner arrived as the ambulance attendants started to struggle with Clay.

"I can't let go, Svetlana," Clay whispered.

"Clay," Tanner yelled. "Lay her down on the stretcher and get in the ambulance."

"I almost lost you," Clay kept repeating.

I touched his wet face, watching as tears and fear etched his handsome face.

"We can't work on her with that giant shoved in there," one of the emergency workers said to the other.

Tanner growled. "Sit on his damn lap, but get her to the hospital. Now!"

I touched my hair and felt the crusty clots of blood.

"Wrong color red." Clay entwined one of my curls around his finger.

My eyes blinked when one of the attendants in white aimed a flashlight close to the iris.

Clay asked, "Is she okay?"

The older guy answered kindly. "They're going to need an x-ray. Her head has stopped bleeding but there's quite a bump."

Clay touched the knot on my head, and I winced.

"Hurts," I said. "I was already out of it, Clay, before Halloway hit me." I rubbed my throat.

"See those red blotches?" Clay pointed out marks on my neck to the older guy. "Choke marks. Damn the bastard to hell."

"He's dead, Clay," Bear said. "He's not going to hurt anyone else ever again. Svetlana made sure of that."

Clay moved over to Bear and actually hugged him. Bear looked uneasy.

"If it wasn't for you getting here before we did, who knows what may have happened to Svetlana. If anything went wrong, I know you would have jumped in to save her," Clay said.

"I'm so very sorry about Gail," I said to Bear. From the moment he had met her, I had an inkling he was sweet on her.

Bear offered a small smile and walked away to where they were loading up Halloway's body.

"You'll probably have to stay the night to make sure there is no concussion," said one of the medics. They finally placed me in the ambulance, with Clay right by my side.

****

My dad and Tennessee were waiting at the emergency entrance.

Dad looked as bad as Clay. He tried to stop the cart, but Tennessee pulled him away.

"Svetlana," Kani called out, worry evident in his voice.

"I'm okay, Dad." I felt woozy, and giddy; most likely the meds they pumped me with.

"They're going to x-ray my head," I called out to my father.

"We'll stay until they let us see you." Tennessee had to answer for my weeping father.

Then I saw her tug on Clay's sleeve as he stood

outside the emergency room door. "She'll be okay."

As I was wheeled away, I heard my dad tell Clay, "Sit down, son, before you fall. You're too damn big for us to pick up."

****

Clay slumped onto a plastic couch. "I shouldn't have let her go into work." He looked up at Kani and his mother. "It's my fault."

Kani sat next to him and patted his knee. "So you're the one that bashed my daughter over the head?"

Clay started to stand, but his mother pulled him back down. "Clay," Tennessee said, "we know what happened."

He looked from one to the other. "It should have been me."

Kani laughed. "You'd be dead. You wouldn't fit in the trunk."

Tennessee giggled.

Clay stared at her.

"Clay," his mother said, "she's going to be all right."

"But it's my fault." For a grown man, Clay couldn't help wanting to cry to his heart's content; instead, he had to sit here and take the blame. "I was so comfortable, eating Mississippi's food, listening to her praise…."

"Praise?" Kani was on his feet. "I lived with that woman for twenty-seven years and she never had a good word to say to me."

Tennessee said, "I think she blamed you for losing Karen."

"God knows, so did I." Kani sat down quietly. He then turned to Clay. "Don't be a fool, Clay. You did

235

not, repeat, did *not* injure my daughter. You've done everything in your power to keep her safe. I knew if I sent her to the mainland with you, I didn't have to worry about a hair on her head.

"Never occurred to me that Tennessee would be shot. Commons must have spotted your MG in the garage. He just shot at anything moving. However, I lost years to guilt about losing Svetlana's mother. Don't take it on.

"That maniac, Halloway, is gone from the world. None of us could have predicted how far his hatred would carry him."

Tennessee spoke softly to Clay. "I'm sorry about your friend, Gail. Captain Tanner said it was a horrible way to die."

Clay hit his chest with his right hand. "Through my fault, through my fault, through my own fault."

"According to Bear, Gail was in love with the man," Kani said. "She had all her defenses down."

"I always suspected Svetlana was right. Halloway did ask for those girls to be killed." Clay's guilt mounted. Right now, he focused and prayed Svetlana was okay. Killing someone would not be easy on her.

****

I talked Kani and Tennessee into going home for dinner, but Clay would not leave my side.

"I think Mississippi would feel better if she could come up and see you," Tennessee said. "I've called her to bring you some ribs and French fries, Clay."

I could see Clay's mouth water. Even with worry, his appetite never disappeared.

"If I could have avoided all this,"—I pointed to my head—"I would have."

Clay stroked my arm. "Why did Gail tell Halloway Chris Manning had shown up?"

"Kani tells me you knew Gail was in love with Halloway." Tennessee's curiosity must have gotten the best of her.

I started to shake my head no, but the pain made me think better of it. "But I don't understand why she thought she loved him."

Tennessee shook her head. "Love does strange things to people."

Kani immediately went to her side.

Tennessee said, "I loved Clay's father, even though I knew."

"Knew what?" Clay asked.

She straightened her chin and faced her son. "That he had no integrity, that he craved excitement, that he didn't love me."

I reached out my arm for Clay, who scooted his chair closer to the bed. "He was nothing like your son," I said.

"No," Tennessee said, "he wasn't. I think the thrill of loving a dangerous man can mix a woman up."

"Did he ever hit you?" I could tell it was the first time Clay had asked. His voice was kept low, forehead creased as though dreading the response.

"No, honey," Tennessee said. "He only broke my heart."

"I'm lucky to know Clay loves me. I think we have to forgive Gail's foolishness. She wasn't given the opportunity to find a good man."

"I didn't know she would be so foolish," Clay said.

Kani immediately got restless. "And God knows you had enough experience with women."

"Now wait a minute," I said. "Who gave you the right to pick on Clay? I will do that in my own time. Tennessee, get him out of here before he says something really stupid."

Tennessee tugged my father out of the room.

Kani came back in to kiss me and pat Clay on the shoulder.

After they left, Clay looked as if Kani had kicked him in the stomach. "Svetlana, do you want to hear about the other women?"

"I've got time for twenty stories." I kissed his hand.

"Twenty?"

"That's what Gail had said."

"She lied," Clay said as if shocked by the fact.

"So, tell me about your love life," I teased.

Clay scratched his head. He took off his rumpled, bloodstained shirt, hung it on the back of the chair, and sat back down with just his T-shirt stretched across the muscles of his chest. "There were only five. I am thirty-two."

"Start with Gail."

"I think she knew I couldn't love her after I found her with someone else."

"Was she always a drunk?"

"Yes, but…."

"Clay, I don't really want to hear about them. I figure you were lonely and some women got closer to you than you wanted."

A look of relief spread over his face. "Yes." Then he sobered. "But I used them, anyway. I wasn't interested in sharing their lives."

"You're only human, Clay." I smiled at him.

"I know you love me," Clay said.
We kissed each other gently with promise.
"I feel cherished," I said.

Chapter Twenty

Friday, December 28

Maui's atmosphere bathed us in sunshine.

Lying on the wicker chaise lounge, surrounded by pillows and inhaling the aroma of Mississippi's flowers, helped erase my lingering memories of terror. I noticed everyone seemed to tiptoe around me. Admittedly, loud noises did startle me beyond my normal responses. The trauma left me exhausted.

The act of killing another human shattered my psyche. I was unaware of the personality trait within me that needed survival enough to obliterate another human being.

Mississippi placed a glass of iced tea, sweetened with sugar and cream, on the table next to my chair. "Doctor said you were lucky to own such a solid skull."

I rapped my forehead with my knuckle. "No concussion."

Clay reached for my hand and held it in his big paw. "You said you remembered the tire iron hitting the gravel next to your face."

"Apparently,"—Kani leaned over to check my eyeballs for the hundredth time—"my daughter's head received a grazing blow."

Tennessee pulled my father away. "Just enough to make it bleed and keep Halloway believing he had

240

finished her off."

Captain Tanner was seated at the patio table next to Bear and Liz Cameron.

I didn't remember how long they had all been there. I kept dozing off from the warmth of the day.

Clay brushed my cheek. "You look awfully good," I said and immediately blushed.

"She's feeling much better." Liz laughed, and the others joined in.

"All nine of the Commons' brothers and their mother are jailed," Bear said as if to chase away any immediate fears.

Tanner shook his head at Bear. "We're not supposed to discuss the case."

Clay said, "I think Bear's right to reassure Svetlana."

He did look good to me. My mouth actually watered. I wanted to be in his arms instead of propped up by the pillows surrounding me.

He wore a light blue cotton shirt over a pair of tan long shorts. His feet wore the sandals that were part of his white silk suit outfit. I measured the width of his shoulders, comparing them to the smaller frame of my father and the larger breadth of Bear's shoulders.

Clay was perfect. Any way you looked at him.

If all these people were not visiting us, I would have asked him to carry me upstairs; to be alone with him, to let him touch me. I pulled his hand to my chest and breathed in the smell of soap on the inside of his palm.

Clay coughed and looked at my father. "They're awaiting trial for arson, murder, attempted murder, embezzlement, withholding information, and a myriad of similar offenses against the state."

Kani was engrossed with encouraging Tennessee to taste one of the apricots we grew in the sideyard.

"Will I have to testify?" I asked.

Captain Tanner waved his hand as if to dismiss any such fears. "I suspect they'll turn on each other shortly. Plea agreements will keep their cases from going to trial. And in your case, it was self-defense. Bear witnessed Halloway getting ready to shoot."

Tanner punched Bear on the shoulder. "We wanted to see that you were feeling better. Not talk about the case. I will promise you I'm determined to keep the brothers separated, even if I have to build two more prisons."

My father knew me well. Both he and Mississippi started to escort the small group of friends indoors. Dad then came back for a hug. "Get some more rest. Maui Power does not expect to see you until the fifth of January."

"What about our wedding plans for New Year's Eve?" I swung my legs over the side of the lawn chair and took a spinning trip in my head even before standing up.

"We may attend Kani and Tennessee's wedding," Clay said, sitting down next to me and holding me securely with his arm around my shoulder. "But I think we should wait until you can walk down the aisle, don't you?"

"Yes," I said. "How long will that take?"

"As long as necessary," Tennessee said. "I'll see you tomorrow at breakfast. Okay?"

I nodded and waved as they left.

Once alone, Clay sat with me once again. "You'll

be right as rain shortly."

"I think I'll stop taking any more pills," I said. "I don't feel any pain. I'm just terribly dizzy."

I leaned back onto the pillows. Clay returned to the house with Mississippi.

I planned to become a detective and be a part of Clay's agency once we married. Yes, I saw what a load of trouble I borrowed, invited into my life, by trying to find out the truth.

Still, the truth did float to the top of the kettle I kept well-stirred. I might not be that bad of a cook, after all. However, I reminded myself that I might need to take a few self-defense courses before I crusaded for another cause.

White-collar crimes were going unpunished.

I could change that!

A word about the author…

Born on a farm in southern Illinois, Rohn Federbush finished her Masters in Creative Writing in 1995 from Eastern Michigan University of Ypsilanti. She started writing full time after retiring as an administrator of the University of Michigan's Applied Physics PhD. Program. Finishing fifteen novels without finding traditional publishers motivated Rohn to self-publish some of her award-winning books. "In Lincoln's Shadow" was a finalist in Daphne de Maurier, 2013 RWA Atlanta Contest. "Maui Time" won third place in 2006 Virginia's Marlene RWA Contest and will be published by Wild Rose Press. "St. Joan's Architect" placed fourth in the 2001 Utah's Heart of the West RWA Contest. The short story "The Prom Dress" received honorable mention in the Iowa Literary Awards in 1999. "The Bus Orphan" was an unpublished semifinalist in the 1997 James Fellowships of Sister, Oregon. Her unpublished memoir-novel entitled "Home from the Woods" mentions her present (fourth) husband, two sons, one granddaughter at Harvard for a PhD in Biological Chemistry and one grandson at Atlanta's Georgia Tech in a Mechanical Engineering PhD Program.

www.rohnfederbush.com